B P Walter was born and raised in Essex. After spending his childhood and teenage years reading compulsively, he worked in bookshops then went to the University of Southampton to study Film and English followed by an MA in Film & Cultural Management. He is an alumnus of the Faber Academy and formerly worked in social media coordination for Waterstones in London.

twitter.com/barnabywalter
facebook.com/BPWalterAuthor
instagram.com/bpwalterauthor

Also by B P Walter

A Version of the Truth

Hold Your Breath

The Dinner Guest

The Woman on the Pier

The Locked Attic

NOTES ON A MURDER

B P WALTER

One More Chapter
a division of HarperCollins*Publishers*
1 London Bridge Street
London SE1 9GF
www.harpercollins.co.uk
HarperCollins*Publishers*
Macken House, 39/40 Mayor Street Upper,
Dublin 1, D01 C9W8, Ireland

1

This paperback edition 2023
First published in Great Britain by
HarperCollins*Publishers* 2023

ISBN: 978-0-00-861871-1

This novel is entirely a work of fiction. The names, characters and incidents portrayed in it are the work of the author's imagination. Any resemblance to actual persons, living or dead, events or localities is entirely coincidental.

Printed and bound in the UK using 100% Renewable Electricity
by CPI Group (UK) Ltd

For Leno

Believe nothing you hear, and only one half that you see.

— *The System of Dr. Tarr and Prof. Fether,*
Edgar Allan Poe

We have such sights to show you!

— *The Hellbound Heart,* Clive Barker

Prologue

I stood very still, trying to calm my racing mind. Trying to focus. Trying to fully understand the choice before me.

The light from the setting sun bathed the room in gold, shining in from the window behind me. The glasses on the table glinted. The smooth polished surfaces gleamed and then, as the sun continued its descent, started to dim.

I can't stay here too long, I told myself. I needed to decide. I knew whatever choice I made wouldn't just affect the person who died. It would change me too. I'd already gone through so much, seen so much. Everything that had happened over that summer felt like it had led me to that moment. The moment I truly held the powers of life and death in my hands.

In the end, I had to take a look. I stepped out into the hall that led towards the veranda. I could see my three choices before me: the person who had brought me here, the elderly man who was nearing the end of his life, or you. *You*, who had occupied my thoughts, reshaped my existence and stolen my heart.

I could have stayed there for hours. Deliberating. Considering my options. Putting off making my decision. But I decided to put a stop to it.

I made my choice.

I prepared the coffee, placing the steaming mugs on a tray. Then I opened the small vial of clear liquid I'd been given.

Less than an hour later, I would have to face the consequences of what I had done. Watch as you closed your eyes, knowing it meant I would never again see their piercing blue depths staring into me. And on my journey across the water away from the island back to the mainland, all I would see was you. The person who entered my world and turned it upside down.

The person I killed.

Chapter One

NOW

I'm sitting by the window when I see you. I had been enjoying a quiet moment of early morning reading with my breakfast, but one of the other guests here – a young woman – got a bit too chatty for my liking, so I decided to relocate. I'm not an unfriendly person, as you know – at least, I don't think I am – but I do like my own company. I've always been good by myself. Good at coping with things, making decisions, sorting out problems. Or I was, until things became difficult and I ended up here.

It's another cold, misty October day and I've gravitated towards the foyer after breakfast for a view of the impressive front lawn and drive. Although I prefer summer, I enjoy the look of the deep, dense mist lying low over the grounds. The scattered dark-brown carpet of leaves across the grass. It's both haunting and beautiful, in its own way. I'm on a comfortably padded window seat and move my gaze to the well-manicured signage marking the entrance: *Wood View Wellness Centre*. I've found focusing my attention on little things – like nature, the view, the weather – a good way to keep my urges at bay. My addiction. The pills I'd purposefully left at home when I came here, locked in a desk drawer, hopefully never to be opened again.

The building is curved, so from my position at the end of the foyer, I can see both the front of the building and down the gravel drive, which disappears into the mist as if there is nothing beyond. Complete oblivion. That's where the car comes from. Oblivion. One moment there's nothing to disturb the view, then shining headlights are breaking through the darkness. It's a taxi, with stickers on the back windows, and I notice it has a dent in the side. It looks rather shabby and ordinary, in contrast to the luxury of this place.

But the person who gets out is anything but shabby and ordinary. Despite the distance, it's clear that your beauty is still there, ready to be appreciated. It's nearly twenty years since I first saw you. Back when we were both twenty-one. Blonde hair, lighter than mine, not curly but not straight either, framing your face – a picture of precise, sculpted perfection.

I almost fall off my seat, and clutch the corner of one of the open curtains, feeling every muscle in my body tense. I hear a ripping sound as I pull on the material, but I don't look up. I don't care.

It can't be *you*.

You can't be *here*.

The secretary at the front desk has been overseeing the refilling of a water cooler, quietly lecturing a younger member of staff on the process. I see her glance my way as she walks back round to the desk. She pauses. 'Are you OK, sir? Is there anything…anything I can get you?'

I shake my head quickly, blinking fast, hoping the crisis within me isn't as visible as it feels.

'It's fine,' I say, as I get up, loosening my grip on the curtain and letting it fall. 'I'm fine.'

I walk slowly but purposefully out of the foyer.

I'm not fine. Nothing could possibly be fine. Not when one is seeing dead people. Or rather person, singular. A person I watched die in front of me on a hot summer's evening on a Greek island, twenty years ago.

Chapter Two

The party was in full swing when my brother Douglas arrived home. Looking around him, he grinned at me. 'Now *this* is more of a party.'

'Yeah?' I said. 'I think I may have invited too many.'

'How do you know all these people?' he said, shaking his head. 'You seem to spend most of your time alone in your room or wandering around the grounds, now suddenly you manage to put on this different hat and be king of the bloody ball. Well, you'd better try to dilute the numbers before Mum and Dad get home.'

I pulled a face. 'Finn and Stephan brought their girlfriends and they brought a group of their friends. It's a bit awkward; some of them I've never even met before.'

Douglas smiled at me sympathetically. He knew I got a little nervous around large groups of people I didn't know. 'And anyway,' I continued, 'what am I supposed to do? Throw people out? I just wanted a small get-together before we're kidnapped and forced to spend the rest of the summer in Greece.'

We walked through the hall towards a group who had gathered in the library.

'Oliver, I must break it to you, but you don't have to come – I think being twenty-one allows you to stay home alone, you know?'

Someone turned up the volume on the stereo from within the connecting living room. Douglas pulled me into the library, laughing, and tried to get me to dance (I *hated* dancing) and when I pulled back and shook my head he stopped. 'Actually, we should talk,' he said. 'Can we go outside?'

I frowned at him. 'Er, yeah, why?'

Douglas didn't say any more – he just opened the French windows, saying, 'Excuse us, sorry,' to a girl we'd both known from our schooldays who had been trying unsuccessfully to catch Douglas's eye ever since he'd walked in. Ignoring her slightly put-out expression, he led me out onto the patio.

'What's this about?' I asked, frowning at him.

'I…just…I don't know…I wanted to warn you about Mum and Dad. Things have been tense since I got back from London.'

'Well, it's probably due to you losing your job and being chucked out of your flatshare,' I said, my memory flitting back to my mother's phone call a few weeks ago, when she complained at me for nearly an hour as I desperately tried to focus on my final university project.

'I wasn't chucked out, I was asked to leave because weird Jeremy decided to move in his stoner girlfriend.'

'OK, OK,' I said, feeling impatient.

'It's not just me, honestly, it's something to do with Dad. He's worried about something, I can tell. He's never been secretive about his work. But he's now having a lot of hushed phone conversations, or going out for long periods of time, even at weekends, and coming back looking worried and irritable and snapping at Mum, which then makes her upset and she gets into one of her states. You know what she's like.'

I sighed. 'Everyone has work stress. Maybe he's worried about money?'

Douglas raises an eyebrow. 'If he is, that would be bad news for us.'

I turn to go back inside. 'Our inheritance isn't our inheritance until it's our inheritance.'

Douglas tutted. 'When did you become all grown-up and understanding?'

'I'm sure everything's fine,' I said, 'but I'll pack plenty of books and suncream, that way I can just ditch them for the beach if their company in the villa gets too stressful.'

Things ended up getting stressful sooner rather than later. As Douglas had predicted, our parents arrived home from their theatre trip to London less than impressed to find the house filled with friends roaming about, drinking beer, getting off with each other and (the worst crime, based on my father's reaction) leaving lit cigarettes balanced precariously on priceless antique furniture.

'Do you know how much that sideboard cost?' my father bellowed, pointing in the direction of the library.

'Don't shout, Hugo,' my mother said, nudging an empty

Budweiser bottle aside with her foot, staring at it as if it were a particularly horrid insect.

'There is a piece of furniture in that room,' he continued, 'that is probably worth more than a small house and I found a *youth* in the library using it as a bloody ashtray! It is now sporting *three*,' he held up fingers to support his point, 'cigarette burns.'

'Sorry,' I said, trying to look suitably chastised, then added, 'How was the Globe? Was Shakespeare worth the four-hundred-year wait?'

'Don't give me that cheek!' he roared. The remaining guests who hadn't vacated the house yet rushed past him. I noticed the young woman from earlier shooting a regretful look at Douglas, who had draped himself over an occasional chair nearby, before she hurried out the front door.

'Oh, I quite liked the Globe,' my mother said, surprisingly brightly. 'Very good seats. Although I've never really understood *Henry V* as much as *A Midsummer Night's Dream*. I told one of the ticket people they should do that one next.'

'Bloody waste of money,' my father barked at her. 'The whole country's going to ruin with those new smirking socialists in charge. And talking of money,' he rounded on me again, 'you can forget about us bankrolling you through a master's if this is the way you act when you come home. Christ, it's like you're still sixteen.'

I'd finally had enough of my father. I turned and walked away from them all, up to the bedroom I'd had since I was a child. Once there I slammed one of the posts of my bed out of anger, tugged off my clothes and fell on top of the covers. I was cross with myself for not predicting this would be how the evening would play out, cross with my parents, cross with the world. Nothing ever changed, I thought as I snatched my pillow and dragged it over my head.

Chapter Three

THEN

I n my bad temper, I was half-expecting to lie awake for
hours, but I ended up drifting off to sleep very quickly. In
what felt like seconds I was being shaken awake by Douglas
saying, 'Oliver, get up.'

I blearily looked at my brother, my vision hazy. 'What do
you want? What time is it?'

'I didn't know you were still asleep,' he said. 'We're about
to leave.'

'What?' I said, jolting upright.

'Get dressed and downstairs as quick as you can. Dad's
about to leave you behind. I woke up late too, but I didn't
know they'd just left you sleeping.'

'I haven't packed,' I said, pulling myself to my feet, 'or at
least haven't finished.'

'I'll go and delay them,' Douglas said as he left the room.

I threw on some clothes as fast as I could, then tugged open
my suitcase that I'd half-packed the day before, checked I had
my passport and then went to my chest of drawers and threw

handfuls of shirts and shorts into my case, along with a stack of random books from my desk.

I found my parents in the entrance hall standing at the foot of the stairs, exactly where I'd left them the night before. If it hadn't been for the blazing sunlight and their change of clothes, it would have been as though no time had passed.

'Why did no one wake me?' I grumbled, letting my suitcase thud down the stairs behind me.

'Oh thank goodness you're here, Oliver,' my mother said. She was in the middle of fastening a long coat, as if she were heading to a Nordic forest in winter and not Santorini in the summer. To say she always felt the cold would be an understatement. 'Your father kept distracting me when I went to wake you.'

'I didn't think you wanted to come,' my father said in a faux-conversational sort of way.

'When did I say that?' I asked, immediately irritated.

My father let go of his own travel case, letting it hit the floor with a loud clatter. 'I've reached the end of my tether. I had to deal with this sort of humiliation all the time when you were at school. I know you say it was just a phase and you were led astray by a bad group of boys and the like, but it wasn't fun to get letters home and phone calls saying you'd gone walkabout in the woods at night or were sneaking around the library after dark – it played merry hell with your mother's nerves.' I could see a red flush starting to illuminate his face in a way that was almost comical, his moustache starting to twitch like a character from a comic strip. I wasn't in the mood for laughing, though.

'Don't blame me,' my mother said, looking mortally offended.

'I'm not at school anymore, Dad, I'm twenty-one,' I said, feeling the stinging prickle of anger rush over me. 'And I'm tired of you still acting like I'm a child you can tick off. Douglas was right – you really are even more tetchy than usual.'

I saw the surprise at my words in my father's eyes. Then they narrowed, hardened and furious, and turned to look at Douglas, who was standing by the front door, just in time to see him mouth *What the fuck?* at me.

'Both of you just take life for granted and presume everything will stay the same,' Dad said, shaking his head. 'You're both in for a shock, boys. Life can chew you up and spit you out.' He picked up his case and marched towards the door. 'The sooner you both learn that the better.'

Mum lingered uncertainly for a moment, looking at us both and then said, 'Well…I'm sure we'll all still have…a nice time.' Then she gathered up her bag and followed our father out of the house.

'Do you think we'll have a nice time?' said Douglas, a slight smile edging the corners of his mouth as he came over to pick up my luggage. He'd always been bigger and more muscular than me and he made carrying two suitcases look as easy as brushing aside a feather.

'I hope so,' I said, sighing. Together we walked out of the house, down the stone steps and over to the taxi waiting for us. We put the cases in the boot and got into the back. Dad made sure the front door was locked then took the seat in the front. Mum was with us in the back. She had taken out a magazine entitled *The Psychic Life* and was busy flicking through the pages muttering something about 'checking the moon cycle'.

We travelled mostly in silence to the airport, with my mother occasionally making the odd comment about something she'd either read in her magazine ('I wonder if I'd enjoy a séance retreat in Eastbourne…') or seen out of the window ('Lovely cows…'). My father just grunted after each one of these, although he did offer up a fact out of the blue at one point about how our family friends the Glovers had recently hired a personal chef for their villa and how he decided to do the same. Douglas and I exchanged looks at this – it was the sort of thing my father would have thought silly under normal circumstances, having a paid chef to serve you omelettes in the morning, but if the Glovers did something it often acquired a gloss of desirability. My father always tried to make us, as a family, tread a line between what he saw as 'unnecessary indulgence' and living comfortably. It was a balance that sometimes defied logic, and my mother rarely got much of a say in the process.

The journey through the airport check-in and into the first-class lounge went smoothly enough. Upon boarding the plane and taking our seats, I was relieved to find I was next to Douglas rather than my parents, although as I sat down my mother reached across the aisle and tapped my arm. 'Oliver, your shoe lace. Don't want you tripping up and falling.'

I knew she meant well, but the comment irritated me and just before take-off, once she was buried in her magazine, I whispered to Douglas, 'Why do they insist on treating me like a child when I'm twenty-one? When will they finally realise I'm a man, capable of making adult decisions?'

Douglas smiled and leaned in to talk quietly into my ear. 'I don't mean this as a criticism because I'm kind of in the same boat, but…well, it might be best to wait until you're less financially dependent on them before asserting this "I'm an adult now" stuff too strongly.'

I didn't respond. Mostly because I knew he was right.

Chapter Four

THEN

Our arrival in Greece was fraught and uncomfortable. My mother's suitcase was temporarily mislaid, causing my father to bark rudely at the airport staff in a way that made me embarrassed to be English while my mum said things like 'Don't make a fuss, dear...I knew a violet-coloured case was a bad idea...it felt...I knew it when I bought it...it felt *unlucky*...'

Things didn't improve when our pre-booked car failed to turn up. Dad started pulling out handfuls of notes he had about the booking details that apparently his receptionist at work had given him and using them to gesticulate at any passing cab driver. 'Bloody useless girl,' he muttered as we climbed into a local taxi after enduring twenty minutes of confusion in the stifling heat. '*Clementine*. What sort of a name is that for a secretary, anyway? I should get rid of her.'

'I rather like clementines,' my mother commented pleasantly.

'Well, it's the last time I'm asking her to sort out my travel arrangements,' Dad grumbled.

The whole journey dragged as I found myself being steadily crushed between the door of the scruffy old Ford on one side and Douglas's legs on the other. The tallest of all of us, he was bent over trying to make himself as small as he could, although the result was fairly ineffective. The taxi driver spoke a language I couldn't understand, but was neither English nor Greek. Despite our lack of understanding, he rumbled away at us, undeterred by our silence, struggling to match the volume of the loud radio, which first belted out 'Vision of Love' by Mariah Carey followed by the selected hits of ABBA.

We were not new to Greece. In fact, we had holidayed on the island of Santorini every year since I could remember. There were times in the past when arriving at our family villa would have been a comfort – the thought of many expansive weeks of sun, sea, nice food and reading. But as I got older, the clean, stark aesthetic of the place had become something of an anaesthetic. There was nothing interesting about it, nor did anything interesting happen in it, aside from an occasional blow-up row between my parents – and even they became tiresome out of sheer repetition.

This year, however, we hadn't even been in the villa for an hour before a vocal disagreement started to kick off. I heard my mother starting to shriek, 'You just don't *care*, do you? You don't care!'

Douglas came into my room more or less instantly. We usually grouped together when this sort of thing happened; it was a throwback to our childhood where we'd sussed out early on there was safety in numbers. Not that our parents were ever particularly nasty to us personally – it was more that their fury and frustration with each other occasionally spilled over, making them likely to start devising chores for us to do or resuscitating old grievances we'd hoped had been long forgotten.

'What's she shouting about?' I said in a low voice as I unfolded an orange shirt and threaded a coat hanger through it.

'Dad's set up a work meeting this evening. Well, a dinner.'

'What, here?' I said, frowning.

'Yes, well, not here exactly, but in a restaurant along the sea front.'

'Just for him – Mum's not going?'

'She's not invited. He's made that clear. Nor are us two, either. Odd, isn't it?'

I sighed, placed the clothes I'd sorted in the cupboard then closed the door. 'Is it? Is this about what you were saying yesterday?'

'Yes – when has Dad ever taken a business meeting on holiday? He always says it's a time to "get away from all that nonsense" and spends his time eating, drinking and burning through a stack of airport thrillers.'

'He takes calls and things,' I said, unpacking the rest of my belongings. 'I don't know; maybe it's just that one of his business contacts happens to be in Greece at the same time.'

Douglas said nothing for a moment, then sat down on the bed with a thud. 'Oh, please yourself. I don't know why you bother getting everything all neat and tidy like that. You're never that bothered at home.'

I laughed. 'It's my way of staying sane in the heat.'

'Fair enough, youngling,' he said, stretching and yawning in an exaggerated way. He'd always called me 'youngling', ever since I could remember, even though there's only a year and nine months between us. I presumed as a child he'd probably heard an adult refer to me in that way and it stuck. Some days I found it endearing, on others it was more than a little annoying.

A loud shout met our ears and then a smash.

'God, what was that?' Douglas said, jolting up.

Together we bolted from the room and down the stairs, the hard floor pleasantly cool on my bare feet. I regretted not stopping to put on my sandals, though, when a few seconds later something sharp dug into my left foot.

'Ah, fuck...' I pulled out a tiny shard of glass that must have made its way onto the bottom stair. The rest of the floor in front of me was covered in fragments, my mum standing above them, crying. I could hear my dad in the direction of the kitchen – it sounded like he was rummaging around for something.

'Mum, what happened?' Douglas asked from behind me.

'Watch where you step,' Dad said, coming in with a dustpan and brush. 'Your mother decided to start flinging glasses everywhere.'

'I didn't *fling* anything,' Mum sniffed. 'I dropped them because I was upset – *upset* that on the first night of our summer holiday, your father doesn't want to spend it with his family. Apparently, he has business to do.'

'It's just a dinner,' Dad said, bluntly, roughly scooping the glass shards into the dustpan.

'Mum, we'll have a nice evening in – we could…go and have a look at the sea, or sit on the terrace,' I said, trying to sound comforting.

I heard Douglas let out a quiet groan. An evening at the villa keeping Mum company certainly wasn't his idea of fun.

'That's sweet, darling,' Mum said, taking out a tissue and dabbing at her eyes. 'Yes, I think I'll do that. Of course, we might starve as we don't have any food and if your father's eating out…'

'You won't bloody starve,' Dad said, straightening up, 'Achilles will be here any moment. I've paid a fortune for us to have a personal chef and he'll have all the food you can wish for and make you anything you want. Plus he'll be living here for the summer so I don't want to hear complaints about going hungry!'

'He's *not* called Achilles?' Douglas scoffed at the same time as I said 'What, he's *living* with us?'

'The Glovers recommended him.' That, apparently, was all Dad had to say on the matter and he went back into the kitchen. A tinny clattering sound suggested the glass had been poured into the bin. Though the floor looked clear, I was still suspicious of its safety, so I turned to go back to my room to get my sandals.

'Oliver, darling, where are you—'

'I'll be two secs,' I called out. I returned as promised and Douglas and I settled Mum outside on one of the loungers by the pool. Douglas fetched her hat, suncream, magazine and books. We tried to make our exit, but she took hold of my hand and said, 'Stay, boys. I want to go through both of your horoscopes for the coming week so that we can plan your routine and activities accordingly.'

Achilles arrived at 4pm and Dad left a few hours later. The man, who looked around thirty, set himself up in the kitchen, unpacking a shocking amount of food from strong woven bags, saying very little, but when he did speak it was with a warm smile. He visited Mum out by the pool, offering her a plate of olives and cheese, which she took, looking at him suspiciously with narrowed eyes, drawing her shawl around her shoulders as if he might suddenly snatch it from her.

Luckily for us, especially Douglas, Mum seemed to have forgotten about any offers I'd made of spending the evening with her. Perhaps her perusal of the horoscopes had tired her, because after our admittedly delicious feta salads served to us by Achilles, she fell asleep in her lounger by the pool.

'Come on, let's get out for a bit,' Douglas said. I was hesitant about leaving Mum at first, worried she'd wake up and go into some loud meltdown about us vanishing. But I was already finding the atmosphere at the villa oppressive and we were only a matter of hours into our stay, so I took the opportunity. We told Achilles, who was cleaning up in the kitchen, that we were heading out for a walk and if our mother asked where we were to tell her we'd be back soon. He nodded, smiled and said, 'No problem.'

'Do you think we're safe leaving Mum in the house with a strange man we don't know?' I asked, suddenly feeling protective of her.

'He's not a strange man,' Douglas said as we walked down

the sloping driveway in the direction of the sea. 'He's Achilles. The Glovers recommended him, hadn't you heard?' He said the last line with mock seriousness and I couldn't help but laugh.

We walked in silence for a while, before Douglas asked, 'Do you think he's attractive?'

I frowned. 'Achilles?'

Douglas nodded.

'Err…yeah, sure.' I felt a prickle of discomfort on my neck. I had told my brother I was gay four years before, when I was seventeen. It was 1993 and there had been a news report on TV about how the British Overseas Territory of Gibraltar had legalised homosexuality. Douglas had been walking through the living room catching the end of the report and just said, 'Ridiculous.' I'd felt my heart start to race and asked 'What's ridiculous?' Douglas had shrugged and said, 'Well, it should have been legal already, shouldn't it?' From that moment I knew my brother was someone I could confide in, and I felt a wave of guilt for not doing so before then. He helped me tell our parents shortly before going to university and to my surprise their reaction was relatively mild. Dad had said, 'Do what you want, it's your body' and my mother muttered, 'Oh, I think the Allertons' son is gay too…maybe I should ask them to pass on some tips…'

In spite of this lack of response or even any interest at all, I'd never really managed to embrace this side of me in a way that seemed to impress, please or reassure those closest to me. I objected to the presumption that I should act in an effeminate way or like certain things simply because I found men attractive, nor did I like people suggesting I must also be prolific in terms of sexual conquests (which was how my friend and flatmate Harold at university always described his own one-night stands with women he'd pick up at one of the nearby student-packed pubs). Douglas frequently – too frequently, in my view – enquired whether there was 'anyone happening at the moment'. I took 'happening' to mean a broad spectrum starting at a fumble outside a club and finishing at lifelong romantic commitment. I usually maintained, as briefly as I could, that nothing was 'happening' anywhere on that front, then would change the subject. But on this night in Greece, as we walked down to the shops and bars and bustle of the coastal stretch where we came every year, Douglas went a bit further.

'Come on, Oliver. You're in your twenties now. They don't last for ever.'

'Don't talk as if you're a wise old man,' I said, 'you're only twenty-three.'

'True,' nodded Douglas, 'but I'm trying to say that it doesn't do to let grass grow under one's feet.'

I gritted my teeth in response but said nothing. I wasn't a virgin, but was acutely aware I was less experienced in both sex and love than most of my friends (and my brother, come to that). But I wasn't in the mood to discuss the topic. I never was in the mood to discuss it.

Our conversation turned to Douglas's sudden eviction from his London flat when he stopped abruptly on the pavement and craned his head towards a window to his left. We were walking past a row of restaurants, set slightly away from the main promenade. These places were more upmarket and much quieter outside than the establishments facing the sea, and as I peered through the window I saw there were only a handful of tables with people at them.

'What are you looking at?' I asked Douglas, trying to get a better view.

'It's Dad,' he said.

'What?'

'Look, there. Table near the back.'

I took his place, leaning forward so I could see to the end of the restaurant. Sure enough, there was our father. And he was with two people, both with their backs to us. A man and a woman.

'Let's go and say hello,' Douglas said.

'What...we can't—'

But Douglas had already dodged past me and opened the front door. Fairly certain this wasn't a wise move at all, I followed him. He'd already begun, rather flirtatiously, to start talking to a young waitress, and his charm seemed to work because in seconds she nodded, smiled and made a gesture that clearly indicated he should go right ahead. I followed my brother as he strode confidently across the floor of the near-empty restaurant to our father. He spotted us before we reached them, a look of wide-eyed panic briefly flickering over his face.

'Dad!' Douglas said jovially, 'We were passing and thought we'd say hello.'

'What? Why? Where's your mother?' he said, looking around jerkily, as if she were likely to pop out of from underneath one of the neighbouring tables as a surprise.

'Back at the house,' I said. 'Achilles is looking after her.'

Dad, frowning, turned his attention back to his table

companions. 'I'm sorry about this. Excuse me, I should take my boys outside for a moment.'

Douglas's eyes met mine for a moment – both of us recognising our shared annoyance about being treated like children. Although, that aside, I was starting to feel embarrassed by this interruption and was about to take my leave when the male guest said, 'Please, do join us.' He shifted in his chair slightly so he could see us, his eyes staring instantly into mine. He was a thin man with dark-brown hair, slightly grey at the edges. His eyes were fixed upon me with a piercing gaze. The flecks of grey in his hair suggested he had passed forty, but other than that it was hard to determine his age.

'That won't be necessary,' my father said, wiping his mouth on his napkin.

'Oh please,' the woman said, she too turning around properly to look at us. 'I'm always keen for some young company.' Her beauty was startling as soon as her face became visible. She looked like a film star or a glossy-magazine model; the kind of person that seems to have a perpetual aura of glamour and sparkle about them. She gave her long blonde hair a little flick with her head so it fell away from her face and when I turned to look at Douglas I could see it plainly on his face: he was completely bewitched by her.

'My name is Argento,' the man introduced himself, 'And this is my partner Nita. We live on an island just off the coast.'

While Nita's accent was clearly American, Argento's was much harder to place; English perhaps, but with a hint of something difficult to detect within the vowels.

'An island? Sounds idyllic,' grinned Douglas.

'Kenneth, your family should visit our villa sometime,' Argento said.

'Definitely,' said Nita.

'I think my sons have been drinking,' my father said, shaking his head, his face now bright red.

'We have *not*!' Douglas replied.

'I think it's time for us *all* to be going,' Dad said.

I saw Argento raise an eyebrow. 'I thought we were going to have coffee,' he said slowly.

'Not possible, I'm afraid.' My father stood up, causing his chair to clatter as the back of it hit the wall behind him. 'We need to get back to our mother – wife! – sorry, their mother, my wife.' He'd taken out his wallet and was scrabbling around inside it, looking disproportionately flustered.

'Do not concern yourself with the bill,' Argento said, laying a hand on Dad's wrist. He snatched it away, as though the man's touch had burned him. 'Fine. I mean, thank you, that's… that's fine. It was nice meeting you both.' With a sharp nod he pushed himself out of the gap between the table and the wall and headed off down the restaurant.

'Apparently we're going,' Douglas said, his eyes on Nita.

'A pity,' she said with the hint of a smile and a slight shrug.

I remained silent as we left, although I thought I felt Argento's eyes linger on me. I had the feeling he was watching me walk all the way to the door, although I didn't turn back and look.

Outside, Dad was incandescent and he and Douglas argued all the way along to the main road, me trailing behind, not wanting to get caught in the crossfire. Usually, I'd be there ready to stick up for my brother, but I felt he'd got us into this situation so he could very well fight his own battle on this occasion.

Back at the house, my mother was still asleep by the pool, although a plate containing a slice of a half-eaten Ravani cake sat beside her, suggesting she had been awake at some point and well tended to by Achilles. The chef himself was nowhere to be seen – I didn't even know which of the guest rooms Dad had given to him.

'Marjory!' Dad said loudly to Mum, causing her to jerk awake. 'We're back. Bedtime.'

'I was already asleep!' she shrieked at him. He apologised for waking her, and reluctantly she accepted this, stopping to collect her belongings before following her husband into the villa and upstairs to their bedroom.

'Fancy a swim?' Douglas said, nodding at the pool once we were alone on the terrace. I was tempted, but suddenly felt a strong tiredness pulling me to my bed.

'Not tonight,' I said, 'I need sleep. Travelling is exhausting.'

'Yeah, I can understand that,' Douglas said, taking off his T-shirt and shorts and jumping into the water in his underpants. 'Christ, it's warm,' he said as he came up for air. 'I think they overheat this thing.'

'Well, take care not to boil alive,' I said. He laughed and began to swim lengths, so I took my own leave.

In my room, I sat in the chair in the corner, feeling exhausted but awake at the same time. Through my window I could hear the swoosh and splash of Douglas in the pool as he did his lengths…the call of a bird…the occasional hoot of a car horn near the seafront. Eventually, I got up and walked over to the window and looked outside. Douglas had finished swimming and seemed to be relaxing at the end of the pool, leaning up against the side, the underwater lights making his outline swirl and sway. A few seconds passed, then he hauled himself out, dripped along the side of the pool and headed inside. I thought about waving to him, but then decided against it, not wanting him to come up to my room and draw me into any conversations about Dad's work stresses or Mum's increasingly unsettled moods. Instead, I looked out further, through a gap in the olive trees, where I could see the soft dunes of the beach and the bright moonlight glint off the sea. And from that sea, you emerged.

The first moment I saw you.

The moon's brightness illuminated the stretch of beach where you were walking, although I couldn't see your face properly, you were too far away. But I wanted to. I knew that. I wasn't sure what it was – perhaps your physique, perhaps the confident way you emerged from the light waves of the sea; whatever it was, I felt an urge within me. An excitement I didn't often have, and when I did I hardly ever acted upon. You picked up a towel from the sand and walked away, the olive trees blocking my view of you. I wondered if, perhaps, you would take the steps up the path that led past our villa.

Without stopping to consider my actions, I went over to my door, opened it and trod as quietly as I could across the marbled corridor to the window at the end that gave a perfect view of the public pathway that led around our property. You came into view almost at once, bathed in the warm light of one of the streetlamps, wearing only dark swim shorts and sandals, a towel slung around your neck. You were beautiful. There was no other way to describe it. I only saw you for a matter of seconds as you walked past, but it was enough to make me aware of my heartbeat.

When I returned to my bedroom, I didn't have any luck with sleeping. But now it was for a different reason. Every time I closed my eyes, I saw you. And I was consumed with the need to see you again.

Chapter Five

THEN

B reakfast the next morning was a tense affair. By the time
I got downstairs, having slept in later than I would
normally, even on holiday, I found my parents and Douglas
having breakfast on the terrace. Achilles was adding dishes to
the already tempting array of fruits, pastries and bread rolls.

'What are these?' I heard my mother ask as I sat down,
interrupting my dad, who was in the middle of saying
something.

'These are *Pischies*, a Cypriot recipe,' Achilles said, 'made
with fried pastry, butter and cinnamon. And in these little pots
you will find crushed nuts and sugar and honey for...' He
mimed taking a pinch and sprinkling it on the top of the
pancake-like pastries.

'Sprinkling?' My mother asked, beaming at him. It was the
first time I'd seen her smile since our arrival – in fact, since I'd
returned from university.

'Exactly so,' Achilles said, grinning back,

'Yes, yes, thank you, thank you,' Dad said, rather rudely I

thought, and Achilles nodded as he returned to the kitchen.

'That was impolite,' my mother said, frowning at him.

'Well, talking of impolite,' my father said, rounding on me. 'I was just saying to your brother here, Oliver, that neither of you are to interrupt a business meeting of mine again. I've never been so embarrassed as I was last night.'

'Oh hang on,' Douglas said, raising a hand to his temple, as if he were receiving some sort of message into his brain, 'Something's stirring…some memory…oh yes, you said exactly the same thing last night in the taxi, and then again when we got home…'

'I've had enough of your sarcasm,' Dad said, a crimson flush starting to spread upwards over his face. I was reminded how he'd looked in the restaurant last night, although there was a slight difference. In this instance, he just looked like he was getting cross, whereas yesterday there was something else in his eyes – something closer to fear.

'Who was that man Argento?' I asked. I pitched the question as if it was conversational and unremarkable, trying to keep a tone of good-natured interest. My father was having none of it.

'Business contact.'

'What sort of—'

'A potential investor,' he said, bluntly, then added, 'Pass the honey. I'm going to try one of these pancake things.'

I did as he asked and dropped my questioning. Perhaps there hadn't been anything interesting in Dad's rather random business meeting. I generally found anything to do with his work rather dull. He worked for a consultancy service in London called Allerton & Quinn. I was never entirely sure about, or interested in, what they did, but I gathered they worked closely with the government (or at least they had before the recent landslide election) and other big businesses from 'a PR and solutions perspective', or so I had heard my father say. All I knew was that his particular role involved keeping the money for the business topped up with contracts and investments.

'What are you two doing today?' my mother asked.

'Beach,' Douglas said, unenthusiastically.

'You could come if you like?' I said to her, trying to sound more welcoming than I felt.

'Oh no,' my mother said, pulling her cardigan closer to her. 'I've never thought open water to be that safe. It's your father's fault for taking me to see that film.'

'What film?' Douglas asked.

'*Jaws*,' she said, popping a kumquat into her mouth.

'Christ,' muttered Dad.

'That was, like, twenty years ago, surely?' Douglas said, laughing.

'I don't see what the timescale has to do with it,' she said, sounding affronted. 'But you boys have fun. I'm sure you could swim faster than me if you ran into any difficulties.'

There were no shark attacks in progress when we arrived at the beach and Douglas and I swam for an hour, then sunbathed. He seemed content to lie and do nothing, whereas I needed some sort of mental stimulation and had brought a battered old Penguin Classic with me.

Having settled ourselves comfortably under the hot Greek

sun for the rest of the morning, we began to feel hungry and realised we'd forgotten to bring any food with us. As we made our way back to the villa, Douglas muttered about lunch, and we were surprised to find a visitor sitting with our mother in the living room.

'Oh boys, you're back,' Mum said. 'This is Nita, the girlfriend of one of your father's business contacts. She's brought us some fruit.' She nodded at the basket in the centre of the table which was practically bursting with colourful items.

'Hello,' Nita said, turning round to look at us, much as she'd done in the restaurant the night before. She was now wearing a casual summer dress, pattered with white and blue lines, and more discreet earrings, although they still sparkled as she did that little flick of her hair once more.

'Hey!' Douglas said, instantly enthusiastic. 'Wow, I mean, nice of you to visit us.'

'I just wanted to drop by and say hello. It's such a lovely day and it was felt that a basket of fruit might be the very thing to make it even better.' Her voice was so smooth, I thought – almost unnaturally so. There was something else unnatural too, although it took me a while to put a finger on it. It was her phrasing. The words 'it was felt' didn't seem natural to her, as if she were an actress performing from a script somebody else had written.

'Rather nice of you,' said Douglas.

'How did you know where we were staying?' I asked. 'And does our father know you're here?' My tone must have been abrupt, as I saw Douglas frown at me.

'He's out,' Mum said with a sniff. 'Needed a break from my

company apparently.' She said it in a way that suggested she had no idea why anyone would desire such a thing.

'And in terms of knowing where you were,' Nita said, 'well, Argento knows everything that goes on around here.'

I stared back at her. She then laughed. 'Relax, I think your father mentioned where your villa was. I'm sure it didn't take much working out.'

I nodded, but couldn't help frowning a little. I felt there was something artificial about her I couldn't identify.

'It's time I should go,' Nita said, getting effortlessly to her feet and striding across the room towards us.

'See Nita out safely and walk her to her car, boys,' my mother said.

Nita laughed again – a cool sound that reminded me of wind chimes – and said, 'I'm sure I'll be fine. And besides, I don't have a car, I walked from down near the beach.'

'I'll come with you,' Douglas said quickly.

I sat down on the sofa as he left the room with Nita. The door thudded shut and I could hear Douglas talking animatedly as they walked away from the house.

'Mum,' I said quietly, 'is Dad OK?'

She looked over at me, her eyes wide. 'Why is everyone so bothered about your father, I'd like to know?' She got up, pulling her shawl off the arm of the sofa. 'Nobody cares about me, do they?'

'Mum, why do you come here year after year if you hate it so much?'

I could tell she was about to flounce off, but she paused for a moment and looked back at me. 'It's the *done thing*, Oliver. You go through life doing one *done thing*, and then another *done thing*, and if the stars align, you might actually enjoy the *done thing*. Like…I don't know…Ascot. But sometimes the *done thing* is very hard. You have to just bundle yourself up, push things down, try not to get upset. That's what my mother always said to me. I'm sure you'll discover how to do that yourself, as life goes on.' She reached in close and for a second I thought, to my surprise, she was about to hug me, but she was just picking out a guava from the fruit basket. Then she went off in the direction of the swimming pool.

'Maybe *I'm* tired of doing the done thing,' I said to myself, with nobody there to hear me.

When Douglas came back, he found me still sitting in the living room, staring at the fruit basket. I wasn't aware how much time had passed, but he seemed surprised to see me there.

'What are you doing?' he asked, closing the front door.

'Nothing,' I said. 'How was your flirtation session?'

'Mock if you will,' Douglas said, good humour in his voice, 'but you have to be proactive to get any action.'

I sat up, looking at him. 'And that's what she is? Action? Even though you're aware she's married.'

Douglas sat down in one of the armchairs, then leaned forwards, tore off a banana from a bunch in the basket and began to peel it. 'She isn't.'

'But I thought—'

'First: she was introduced to us as that guy's partner, not wife. Second: that's not even the case, it turns out.'

'What do you mean?'

Douglas took a deep breath. 'Well...she's sort of...a paid escort.'

I stared at him. 'A prostitute?'

'Hmm...' He tilted his head. 'That's a rather...unpoetic word.'

'What would be more *poetic* for you?'

'Oh, come on, Oliver. You may live a life of chastity but you must know how the world works.'

'I don't doubt how it works, I'm just not sure she's the sort of woman you should be getting mixed up with.'

'*Sort of woman?*' Douglas frowned. 'That sounds disappointingly narrow-minded.'

'I don't mean it like that.'

'She's an actress – or wants to be – and rich men pay her to be their girlfriend at work events and parties or even for her company, and to stay with them for periods of time. She's with that fellow Argento for the summer.'

'Right,' I said. 'Well, I hope you worked out all your contractual terms and conditions and she's giving you a competitive rate.'

'Don't be silly,' he said. 'Surely you know what it's like to see someone and just...just *want* them. And when that happens, everything else becomes white noise in the background.'

I didn't answer. My mind had flicked back to the evening before, when I'd watched you through the hallway window. When I'd seen your face for the first time.

'Think what you like, Oliver,' Douglas said, getting up, 'but you're the one who's going to be lonely all summer. Not me. Not if I can help it.'

Chapter Six

THEN

That evening, I continued to find everyone very grating. Mum spent most of dinner complaining about being 'left alone to greet our guests'. Douglas pointed out it was just one guest, which didn't go down well. Dad seemed disconcerted about Nita's visit to the villa and had taken to questioning us all in detail about what she said and how long she was here for. He seemed troubled by the idea of Douglas going for a walk with her, too, and said, 'Just don't get any ideas.' When Douglas asked what the hell that was supposed to mean, Dad went temporarily deaf and started criticising the wine Achilles had served us. When silence descended, my mother muttered how it was 'starting to get a bit chilly' and that she suspected 'winter was on the way'. The statement was so ridiculous, that as the rest of us sat there sweltering in the July heat, I would have found it funny if I hadn't been in such a bad mood.

Eventually, I made my excuses to leave, saying I was going for a walk to 'clear my head'. I made my way down the path towards the sea, kicked about near the water's edge, then returned to find my parents in the living room watching television and Douglas swimming.

'What are you watching?' I asked.

'It's *awful*,' my mother said, as if this told me everything I needed to know.

'I might go to bed,' I said.

'Night,' Dad grunted from the armchair nearest the screen.

But I didn't go to bed. Like the night before, I felt unable to rest, although this time I felt I had more energy, as if I wanted to do something, something exciting, away from the depressing mundane repetition of the past few days in the villa, all of us getting on each other's nerves. In the end, I picked out a smarter shirt and trousers and went quietly downstairs and out through the side door.

Instinctively I made my way towards the seafront, walking down past the other nearby houses, the scent of the lemon trees and jasmine plants filling the night air around me. When I got to the shore, I found myself uncomfortably hot despite the cool sea breeze, and felt a sudden urge to jump into the water. But I didn't. My attention was caught by a couple crossing the road.

It was Nita. Her arm was linked through Argento's. They looked relaxed, Nita in the same long black dress as the night at the restaurant. Perhaps they were off out for another dinner. For a second, I wondered if my father would materialise from somewhere. I decided to follow them, just out of interest, to see where they went.

It didn't take long. Within less than a minute, they walked into one of the bars on the seafront – a less luxurious location than where I'd first seen them. I lingered outside for a moment, trying to see if I could spot them through one of the scuffed windows.

'You want smokes?' a man asked, coming up to me, offering a pack of cigarettes.

'Err... no...I'm...I'm going inside.' I wasn't sure why I announced it, but having done so, felt I had no option but to do just that. Inside the music was loud and people were bustling around, drinks in hands. It took a moment to spot them. They'd squeezed into a table in the corner, away from the bar. I didn't want them to see me, so I took a stool on the other side of the bar, far enough away that I'd be unnoticeable but just close enough that I could keep an eye on their conversation.

'Drink?' the woman at the bar said, flashing me a grin.

'Yes, thank you, I'll get – oh, sorry, you were first.' The person who had sidled up to my left turned to look at me, hands out, signalling I should place my order.

It was you. Standing there, right in front of me, in a red shirt and light beige shorts. A jolt ran through me. I recognised your face as if I had known it all my life, not just glimpsed it as you walked underneath a streetlamp late at night. Your beauty was like radiation. I was speechless, breathless, the skin on the back of my neck prickled.

'I...I...' I stammered, unable to find the words.

'You were going to get a drink?' you said, slowly, smiling a little. 'I'm sorry, I didn't mean to push in.'

Your accent was English. Rounded. Well-spoken. Similar to mine, although deeper. It had almost as much of an effect on me as your looks.

'You're not…' I said, in almost a whisper. 'I meant… sorry…' I tried to speak up, 'You're not pushing in. I'm…I'm still choosing.'

The sentence sounded silly to me and I regretted not being able to come out with something smoother, cooler, something that would charm you, make you think I was intelligent, fun, worthy of your attention. This was the sort of thing Douglas was much better at than me. 'I…should go,' I said, feeling my face going red, turning away.

I walked out of the bar. You followed, putting a hand on my shoulder as soon as I'd gone through the door. 'Wait,' you said, 'are you OK?'

'Yes. Sorry.'

'Stop saying sorry,' you said with a little laugh, 'you haven't done anything to be sorry about.'

I laughed too. 'Very true.'

'Why did you leave?'

I shrugged, trying to let my breath out naturally. 'I wasn't even sure if I wanted a drink.'

'Then why were you in there?' You asked the question simply. I didn't feel this was an interrogation. You seemed actually interested. I didn't feel I could tell this stranger I was following two other almost strangers and didn't really have any justifiable reason to do so.

'I was…out for a walk and thought I'd…just…go for a drink.'

The first time speaking to you, and I was lying. Telling you untruths. I tried to dismiss this thought, thinking it didn't matter. All that mattered was that I begin to sound more like a normal, coherent human being.

'Well, let's go for a drink.' You said it simply, easily. 'But somewhere else. That place is too loud.'

I smiled at you. 'OK, I'd like that.'

You started to lead the way, then looked back into the window of the bar, then tapped your pocket. 'I think I've left my wallet inside. Two seconds.' You nipped back in through the door, skirting around a couple who were coming out.

Once you were back, you led the way to a smaller, quieter bar, about a ten-minute walk down the row of shops and restaurants. It was dark inside, with deep-red walls, and only a few other people standing around. We sat at a table, you bought me a beer, and we started talking,

I was taken aback by your sudden, incautious honesty. You were so unshakingly confident I'd want to know about your life, what your plans were, how you'd come to be in Greece. And I did. I wanted to know all of it.

It turned out you were an orphan. You had recently lost both your parents when they were travelling in the Middle East for your father's work. A bomb had taken out the front of the hotel where your parents were staying. I said I was sorry, but to my surprise you shrugged and said, 'I wasn't close to them. To tell you the truth, I barely saw them.'

You explained how you had inherited a portion of your family's wealth on your twenty-first birthday, and would inherit the whole lot in three years when you turned twenty-five.

'My family didn't put too many conditions on my use of the money, but they didn't want me having too much of it before I was in my twenties. Presumably to stop it going to my head. I have enough to live on. But it does mean when I travel, I have to stay in hostels, not Hiltons. For now, at least.'

I never got the feeling you were boasting or showing off – it was all put forward conversationally but lacking any major emotions. Occasionally you smiled and laughed a little, but mostly you kept your facial expressions hard to read – or not there at all. A quiet intensity I found deeply attractive. So I sat back and listened to the flow of information.

'I have some relatives in Greece,' you continued. 'They invited me to stay with them, but I always have this need to be in the centre of the action. Another reason why a hostel was a good choice.'

'As in one for…like…backpackers?' I worried after I'd said it that I would sound snobbish, but you seemed unbothered.

'Yeah, very basic. I'm in a dorm room that sleeps three, although the other two beds are unoccupied at the moment, which is good. Where are you staying?'

I said I was in a villa nearby with my parents and brother. I told you how dull I found it, how suffocating the atmosphere was. How I needed a break, needed to get away.'

'So you're…looking to get away for the night?' You raised your eyebrows, just a little.

I felt my heart rate start to quicken once more. 'I…suppose,' I said, looking at him, holding his gaze.

You moved in your seat slightly, bringing yourself forward. As you did so, your knee made contact with mine. You let it stay there.

'Have you ever seen the inside of a backpackers' hostel?' you asked. Your voice had dropped even lower. Even quieter. But I could still make it out, my eyes trained on your lips.

46

'No.'

You nodded slowly. 'Well, perhaps we should remedy that.'

'Perhaps we should,' I said. My throat felt tight. My hands hot. But I knew what I wanted. And you knew that I knew.

'Come on, finish your drink,' you said.

I smiled nervously and did as I was told.

Chapter Seven

NOW

I go straight back to my room. As I walk along the corridor, my brain refuses to stop turning, churning, desperately trying to make sense of what is happening.

How can you be alive?

Wouldn't I have known it all this time?

And if you are alive, why are you here? It can't be coincidence, can it? *Can it?*

I walk as fast as I can manage, ignoring the staff or guests who turn to look at me. When I am metres from the door to my room, I trip and feel myself flying forwards, unable to find anything to hold onto. I crash to the floor, the skin of my knuckles scraping the corner of the open door of a store cupboard. Dizzy and furious with myself, I scramble to my feet. The door closes.

'My gosh, are you OK?'

It's the chatty woman from breakfast. I would have sighed with irritation if I'd had the breath to spare.

'Fine, I'm…sorry, I…'

'Don't apologise, did you hit the door? I'm so sorry if it was my fault, I was looking for some extra conditioner. I know this is the men's wing, but the store cupboard on the other side didn't have any. Don't you think it's weird they separate us by gender, in this place? Anyway, you know they give us a set of shower gel, shampoo and conditioner when we arrive – well, they've continued to replace the empty bottles of the other two, but not the conditioner, and it's bloody annoying, I must tell you.'

She has a warm, friendly voice, something I hadn't noticed at breakfast when I'd been trying to read. Something about her presence calms me and I manage to smile a little. 'Ah, yes, that is annoying.'

'Has it happened to you?' She frowns.

'Well, I just use the shampoo and shower gel in the things on the walls in the showers. I don't have an en-suite. Not rich enough for that.' I let out an awkward laugh that echoes around the empty corridor in a disconcerting sort of way.

'Ah, I see,' she says, still smiling. 'Are you sure you're all right after your fall? You're sure you – oh gosh, you're bleeding.' She pointed at the knuckle of my right hand. I looked down at it and saw I'd broken the skin as my hand had hit the door.

'It's nothing,' I say, suddenly feeling like I need to get past and get to my room. But she steps forward and takes my hand in hers. 'Let me see,' she says, her smile changing to a furrowed brow of worried concern. Her brown hair falls over her face a little and I find myself looking at the lines on her face. I had presumed she was in her twenties, but now I decided she must be over thirty. The sound of someone climbing the stairs from the landing behind me makes me start and I pull my hand away.

'I really must get to my room,' I say. Before she can say anything, I've skirted past her and continue up the corridor until I get to my door. I tap the key card on the pad and let myself in.

I slump in the entrance to my room once I've closed the door, then all but crawl towards my bed. Once I've reached it, I can't do anything for a minute or two. I don't get into the bed, I just sit on the floor up against it, trying to calm myself down. I need to breathe slowly, I need to centre myself.

I need some pills. Desperately.

I feel a pain spreading across my back as if someone has poured a mug of hot water over my shoulders. I don't know if this is me imagining it – if the addict part of my brain is trying to convince me I am in need of painkillers. Or if it's just where I've jarred myself when I fell. I have no way of knowing. I'm not in a fit state to think clearly. And as the minutes go on, all I can see is your face. Burned into my mind. Always there somewhere, but now at the forefront. Back in the present. Still alive.

I don't leave my room the whole day. I swing from maniacally trying to make sense of the situation, to work out what happened, how it's possible for you to be here, to then deciding I'd just imagined it, and it was my unconscious mind projecting a face from my past onto the body of a total stranger.

Or what if you've come here to find me? I think to myself as I tug off my jeans and shirt and get into bed, pulling the covers around me.

How can I ever leave this room again? How can I risk it? How will I go on living without knowing for sure whether you were here or just a trick of my mind – a symptom of my addiction withdrawal?

All these thoughts remain my unhappy company as I drift in and out of sleep. I remain in bed for most of the day. I don't go to any of the group therapy classes or exercise sessions I've attended during my two weeks here. They're optional anyway. The staff aren't strict here. It's not one of those rehab clinics you see in movies where you get ordered around like it's school or a posh prison. Things are calm. There's help if one needs it, classes to attend, a lot of them based on talking therapies, cardio exercise or mindfulness. But it's very self-guided. Nobody's strong-arming anyone into anything. Guests come here for specific help, or for the quiet and relaxation of the grounds. Although it seems unlikely I'll be getting any of the latter now.

At 3pm I get out of bed and turn on the television. I flick through channels and end up in the middle of some chat show about iconic fashion photography. This doesn't interest me so much and I'm about to change the channel again before a face fills the screen. The face of a woman.

It's a coincidence – of course, it is. Her face is everywhere, all the time. It's strange, but when you want to avoid something, it somehow becomes so present you feel as if it's chasing you, hunting you.

I pick up the remote and jab it at the screen but it doesn't respond and it takes me a moment to realise I'm holding it the wrong way round. *Fuck,* I curse, as her face remains on the screen, then changes to a new photograph, that famous shot of her on a diving board, sitting right at the end. The voiceover on the television programme starts to say how the photo was taken shortly before the subject's death in the summer of 1997 and goes on to comment on the choice of swimwear and how it could have impacted sales at the time of similar items. I finally get the TV off, just as they change to an earlier shot of their subject wearing, according to the narrator, 'the black sheep wool jumper by Warm and Wonderful'.

In the silence and the gloom, I wander around, unsure what to do. I'm getting hungry, having missed lunch, but I don't want to go down to the café to get food. You might be there. Waiting.

In the end, I decide I can't remain prisoner in my room and opt to take a shower, hoping it will jolt me out of the state of unease I've found myself in.

Wood View Wellness centre has three 'tiers' when it comes to cost and quality of stay. The lowest tier – my tier – was more like a hostel experience (albeit with more luxurious bedding and a room and TV to oneself) separated by gender on the ground floor, with men in the west wing of the building and women in the east.

So many things over the years have reminded me of my summer in Greece. So many things have brought the past crashing into the present. References to world events in 1997. Moments that happened in the Before – my graduation, moving back home. And then After. Leaving Greece and going back to England. Trying to move on with my life. Sometimes succeeding. Sometimes failing. But nothing that's happened since could have prepared me for what's happening now. The disorientation and panic I felt this morning when I saw a dead man walking. The question that now sits heavy upon me: *What if you'd never actually died?*

I leave my clothes on the white bench and head for one of the cubicles. As the water cascades down I push the button on wall on the shower gel dispenser.

The shower area has warm, inviting lighting – bright, but not in a harsh, fluorescent sort of way. It causes the frosted glass dividers to glow and flicker as the water starts to cascade around me. At first, I thought the shadow, the moment of vague movement, was just this combined effect of light and water. But then the light is blocked behind me. That's when I know someone is standing right at the opening of my cubicle.

I keep swallowing. I remember hearing on a radio interview with someone who had a habit of feeling faint or dizzy that swallowing helped ground him. I try this now, willing myself to keep calm, even though I know deep down that you're standing there.

'Hello, Oliver,' you say, simply.

I open my mouth. I manage to speak.

'Hello, Alastair.'

We look at each other for a long time, me standing in the shower, the water flowing over me, my vision occasionally obscuring. I don't brush it out of my eyes, or push my fringe back, or step out of the cubicle. For a long time, I just stare. And you stare right back. A dead man, made real. Although clearly older, as I noticed when I saw you get out of the car from the window, you are still relatively unmarked by the deeper cuts of age. Your face is still mostly wrinkle-free, your skin still has the youthful smoothness of a man in his early thirties rather than early forties. Your hair is cut shorter than you used to have it, but still thick on top and of the same dark-blonde hue. The same as mine. I can't help but think it: you remain the most beautiful being I could ever hope to see. And your presence devastates me.

I suppress everything I want to ask. Every question rushing to the surface, threatening to push so hard at the front of my mind. It's all I can do not to scream them at you. *How? Why? What now?*

I know one of us must speak soon. I need to get to the bottom of what is going on here. But before any kind of discussion can occur, I hear the footsteps and the sound of the door opening – the sound I'd missed when you had entered the room. I hear movement at the other end near the benches – presumably whoever it is is hanging up a towel – and then a young man walks into view. He's slim and toned, younger than me, and if this had been a different situation, a different circumstance, he's the kind of guy I would have been interested in. He walks slowly around you, clearly confused by a man standing fully dressed in the shower area. But he doesn't say anything – just goes into one of the cubicles opposite and starts the shower. Every now and then, as he washes himself, he glances back over to us. This standoff can't continue for ever and eventually I shut off my shower and come to a decision. 'There's a seat in the garden, round the back of the building, underneath a large oak tree. You'll see it from the terrace. Meet me there in fifteen minutes.'

With every ounce of effort I can summon up, I step out onto the wet tiled floor and walk past him. At the bench I pause to wrap the towel around my waist, bundle my clothes into a ball and set off back to my room.

Back in my room, I throw everything onto the floor and sit down on my bed, putting my head in my hands. I let a half-gasp, half-sob escape me. I run my hand through my still soaking wet hair and try to calm myself. Once my heartrate has begun to return to normal, I roughly towel myself dry.

The cold autumn air hits me as I step outside ten minutes later. There are a few people sitting on the terrace, talking amongst themselves, mugs of coffee or tea clasped close. There's a woman sitting away from them, older and morose looking, a paperback book on her lap, unread and untouched, her gaze staring off across the mist-shrouded lawn. I recognise her – she's an actress, big in the 1980s in US comedy dramas. I'd heard she'd had a problem with alcohol in the past. Maybe things had got bad again. Things can always get bad again. I know that very well. How seductive those lies can be; the lies you tell yourself. That you'll never regress. Never go back. Then you feel that tug, reeling you back in. Slowly at first, sometimes hard to spot. Then with a force that takes your breath away.

I think about the pills back home in my desk drawer.

Then I think about the island.

Shaking my head, trying to dismiss my thoughts, I walk off the concrete and onto the grass. Although there's been rain this week, the ground feels surprisingly firm as I tread towards the oak tree, my feet rustling through the dropped leaves that have been blown across the grass. I can see you sitting there. You're early. Watching me approach.

I sit down next to you.

Silence remains between us for almost a full minute. Then, at last, you speak. 'Why aren't you saying anything?'

I open my mouth and say aloud the sentence I have been rehearsing on my walk over. The sentence that threatens to break me apart if I don't get an answer to the central question behind it.

'I'm waiting for you to tell me how you're still alive. And why you haven't contacted me for over twenty years.'

Chapter Eight

THEN

I woke up to dazzling sunlight streaming through the curtains. For a moment I was confused as to where I was and jolted up, feeling disoriented and panicked. Then I felt movement next to me, something up against me. It was you. We were in bed together. I was in a dorm at the hostel where you were staying. Last night all came back in a sudden, breathtaking rush.

How you'd led me past the girl on reception, who hadn't commented. How you'd taken me into the dorm room, pulled me over to your bed and drew me in, your lips finding mine. Your clothes falling to the floor. Mine falling to the floor. Then you pushed me down on the bed. Your strength and confidence as you guided me to do what you wanted – and because you wanted it, I did too.

The thoughts of our activities the night before left me feeling dazed and strangely unreal, as if an actor had strode into the room at some point and taken my place. But I couldn't help it. The more I thought about it, the more I smiled and lay back next to you as you continued to sleep.

You woke up not long after I did, stirring a little and then pulling yourself up on your elbows to look at me, strands of your blonde hair hanging down over your eyes. You seemed even more beautiful in this dishevelled, naked state, and I couldn't resist, couldn't wait to say good morning – I pulled you towards me and we embraced, as though falling into a deep ocean, hands caressing faces, legs entwining around each other's frames. Eventually we stopped, realising the day had begun and we had better get out of bed and face it.

'I should get back,' I said, getting out of bed, feeling the inevitable encroachment of real life start to stain the joy of our time together. 'My parents will wonder where I am if I'm not home soon.'

I looked out of the window and watched the seafront start to come to life, the fishermen arriving back, the early-morning tourists, those out to get breakfast or heading to the beach before anyone else got there. I turned back to you. You were sat at the edge of the bed, as naked as I was, the light illuminating your golden skin. 'Stay,' you said, quietly.

I let out my breath, feeling my body react to the sight of you. I stepped forward, reached out to touch your shoulders. 'I really should go. My mother…she'll…she'll panic if I'm gone.'

I noticed the slightest frown crease the edge of your temple. 'Oh, come on. I thought you were twenty-one, not seventeen.'

You didn't say it unkindly, just with a mixture of playfulness and plain truth. I stared at him, and he stared back. 'Let's go and get some breakfast,' he said.

I went with him. I knew I would. I knew there was little

point trying to resist those deep, hazel eyes or that small but irresistible smile. So we went for breakfast at a café you seemed familiar with. It was close to the hostel but further away from my family villa and I felt a vague tug within me as we took our seats and ordered food – that feeling when you know you're probably doing the wrong thing, but carry on anyway.

Little did I know it at the time, but that feeling would come to define my time with you that summer.

There was indeed hysteria when I returned home to the villa. My disappearance had been discovered and I let myself in just in time to hear my mother shriek, 'Check the swimming pool – he may have fallen in and drowned in the night!'

I went through to the outdoor terrace to assure them all I hadn't 'drowned in the night'.

'Where were you?' my father asked gruffly, 'You've caused your mother to get all wound up. We probably won't have a moment's peace for the rest of the week because of it.'

I turned to my mother, who was making her way over to me. 'I'm sorry, Mum, I…I woke early and couldn't sleep, so I went for a morning walk.'

She dabbed at her tears with a tissue. 'Your brother said your bed hadn't been slept in.'

I looked over at Douglas, who was sat on one of the sun loungers eating a pastry. He mouthed *Sorry* at me.

'Well, he was wrong. I just made it before I left. Keep things tidy, as you always say.'

She sniffed and wiped her eyes again. 'I suppose.'

Once things had calmed down and Mum had settled in a seat by the pool, draped as ever in a shawl and perusing the horoscope pages in her magazine, Douglas sidled over to me. 'You, um, weren't out for a morning stroll, were you?'

I shook my head.

'*Bad boy*,' he said, in a low voice, and laughed.

'Let's not,' I said, feeling embarrassed, but couldn't help returning his grin.

Perhaps this holiday wasn't going to be so dull after all, I thought to myself, as I headed back inside.

I had arranged to meet you by the sea. The fact you'd invited me for breakfast suggested to me our activities the night before hadn't been a one-night thing and I was delighted when you asked me to meet you on the stretch of beach directly down from my villa at 1pm. I did as you asked, although immediately requested we walked further down along the sand, mindful that my parents might see us from an upstairs window and start asking questions.

We walked back down along the curvature of the beach towards the promenade of shops and restaurants. We swam in the sea when we came to an empty stretch of sand, away from both boats and other swimmers. You frequently pulled me in close to you and tried to kiss me, although I felt more shy here, in broad daylight.

At one point, when I became hungry, I glanced towards the shoreline, noticing that we were being watched. There was a man drinking a coffee, at one of the small barista stalls, very clearly facing us. Watching. With a jolt, I realised who he was.

'Who are you looking at?' you asked, following my gaze.

'Don't look now,' I said, worried you'd draw attention to us, 'but that man over there – I met him earlier this week. At a restaurant.'

Your eyes widened a little, 'Did you indeed? And what happened on this night, may I ask?' There was a glint in your eye. Something slightly mischievous that made me grin back.

'Nothing,' I said, keeping my voice quiet. 'It wasn't like that.'

'I'm pleased to hear it,' you said, swimming over to me. 'I wouldn't want to be getting jealous, would I?'

I returned your smile and continued, 'It was…well, a sort of business meeting my dad was having. My brother and I gate-crashed it. But there was something rather strange about him.'

'Strange?' you asked, casually floating around so you could follow my gaze.

'Yes,' I said, 'strange. It's hard to say. Maybe I imagined it.'

'Well, let's find out,' you said, looking back at me.

'What?' I asked, suddenly worried.

'Perhaps we should say hello.'

And with that, you began to swim to shore, me following, feeling both surprised and uneasy.

Chapter Nine

THEN

'Hello again,' Argento said when we stepped out of the sea and walked towards him. I couldn't help watching Alastair's graceful exit from the water, the droplets on his skin glinting as he moved.

'Hi,' I said, trying to focus. 'Nice to see you again.' I wasn't quite sure if 'nice' was the right word. I was still far from certain that I wanted or needed to talk to this man, but I hadn't wanted to seem unfriendly or standoffish, especially when you had decided we should say hello.

'I was hoping to see you again. Nita mentioned how welcoming you and your mother were,' he said. 'And your brother, of course.' I assumed this was a reference to Douglas and Nita's walk together. I wondered how much she had told this man, whether any of her actions could be put down to free will or were simply instructions he had given her. It made me feel strange to think of an actor of sorts coming into our midst.

A beat of silence passed, then he looked over at you,

standing patiently, watching us. I suddenly felt awkward and began to introduce you in a clumsy, stammering sort of way.

'It's a pleasure to meet you,' you said, shaking the older man's hand.

'My name is Argento.'

'That's an unusual name,' remarked Alastair. There was something in his eyes – amusement, perhaps – that caught my attention. But before I could think about it properly, Argento spoke again.

'I have been doing business with Oliver's father. It is my hope that we're close to reaching a very lucrative agreement for us both.'

I nodded, not having anything to add on this subject. I remembered the unsettled way my father had behaved when we discovered him with Argento and Nita in the restaurant. It didn't sit well with me. I felt out of my depth. In the dark. And this feeling continued when he then asked 'May I buy you boys lunch?'

I opened my mouth, closed it again, then glanced at you.

'That sounds great,' you said, with an instant nod that surprised me.

'Are you…sure?' I asked, under my breath.

'Why not?' you shrugged.

'I'm not sure my father…' I started to say, though couldn't think of a polite way of finishing it.

'Your father is busy with paperwork, I'm sure,' Argento said, not fully grasping what I was about to say, or perhaps choosing not to.

'That's settled then,' you said. 'We'll dry off and get ready.'

I found myself nodding, smiling back at you. The truth was, I was so in your thrall, you could have suggested almost anything and I would have gone with you and tried my best to be happy and willing about it.

Argento led us down past the coastal restaurants, making me think we were going to sit at one of the outdoor tables in the sun. But to my surprise, he took a turning off the main road, down a narrow passageway into the heart of the old town, keeping to the winding back streets until we came to a small restaurant with a red sign outside that simply said 'Sunset'.

'This is one of the best restaurants in this part of Greece,' Argento told us, then walked inside.

The food was indeed superb. I had an artichoke and lamb moussaka with a rich and distinctive flavour. You and Argento both had meatballs with roast vegetables. We chatted about art and books and wine (Argento had chosen us a bottle to share). I didn't notice then that Argento gave precious little away about himself, letting you and me talk while he sat back and offered occasional prompts. We told him about our lives, our families, why we were in Greece, what we'd been doing. Afterwards, when we made our way out into the shady late-afternoon streets, Argento put in another request for our company.

'I would like you both to come to my villa. It's situated on an island just a ten-minute boat ride from here. I will have a man pick you up at the jetty by Marco's Bar at seven on Saturday evening. Would that suit?'

I was taken aback and didn't say anything for a few seconds. Argento seemed to guess what was concerning me. 'I could, if you wish, extend the invitation to your family. Your father, mother and brother could join us, perhaps?'

He glanced, very briefly, over to you, before returning to me. It was clear he had sussed out that I didn't want you exposed to my family, or for them – or my parents at least – to know of your existence. Perhaps he thought I was ashamed of being gay, or maybe he suspected that I wasn't ready to share you with anyone just yet.

'No,' I said, a little too quickly, 'I...don't think that's necessary. To invite them, that is.'

I look over at you to get a sense of your reaction. I'd started to learn, though, that few things ever seemed to surprise you – or at least you didn't really show it. You just pushed some stray blonde strands of hair away from your forehead and said, 'Sounds good to me.'

I immediately started to nod, even if I didn't quite know what we were getting into. 'Sure,' I replied, trying to sound equally casual.

'I am pleased,' Argento said, coming to a stop before the road opened out onto the main seafront. 'I'm a firm believer in taking a leap into the unknown. I feel the sunshine of Greece has a special magic to it that makes the impossible seem suddenly quite possible. I'm sure you will both will see what I mean when you visit my villa. It is extremely beautiful.'

He then turned and walked away. We watched him until he was out of sight. His exit was odd; it left me wondering why he didn't say goodbye or ask which direction we'd be going in.

'That was all a bit…well…strange,' I said to you as we started our journey back to the beach.

'I liked him,' you replied. 'I wonder what his villa is like.'

'If Argento's company has been anything to go by,' I said, feeling a little uneasy about our plans, 'I think we should expect the unexpected.'

Chapter Ten

THEN

I worried you would soon grow tired of me, as the days passed, but you showed no sign of it. Even though you said you weren't one for making plans, you didn't seem averse to a routine, albeit a loose one. We ended up spending the next few days in much the same way, once I had escaped from my parents, which wasn't always easy. We had breakfast on the seafront, then swam in the sea, or went for walks in the nearby countryside that snaked around the villas and small hotels in the hills. It had become quite amusing to us that the young woman on the desk at the hostel never seemed to notice an extra, unofficial resident going past her for a bout of afternoon sex or, on occasion, to spend the whole night in one of the beds meant for paying guests. At times I wondered what it would be like if I brought you back to my parents' place and introduced you as... as what? My new boyfriend? Someone I was 'hanging out with'? Sleeping with? Part of the problem in such a scenario was a question of how to define our relationship, which I had to remind myself was still in a very nascent stage. What if any attempt at definition made you feel insecure, suffocated, caused you to run away? The thought made my stomach lurch, as though I were staring down at a great drop with the end out of sight. So I kept you more or less a secret, though I suspected Douglas may have made allusions to what I was getting up to on the nights when I didn't come home, which was a surefire way to make my parents look the other way and avoid asking too many questions. Such a reaction was certainly an improvement over hysterical assumptions that I had drowned.

During our days together, we talked surprisingly little, although when we did talk it was often led by you rather than me. I had a slight suspicion I didn't quite match up to your intelligence or interest. If I raised a topic of discussion, you often ended up looking away into the distance, as if something had caught your eye, or became preoccupied with sand on your swimming trunks, then changed the subject soon after. In anyone else, this would have put me off, but with you it felt like a challenge.

Most of the time, though, we read books, lying side by side next to each other, our arms touching. I noticed you easily read volumes of literature and philosophy in French and Greek, and occasionally I would try one of the books you finished, although my French proficiency was nowhere near as good as yours – something I wasn't keen to let on – and I probably ended up taking away only a vague understanding of the story or messages within it. We found a small second-hand shop that sold antiques as well as paperback novels – a curious assortment of literature new and old, much of it in English, perhaps leftover or donated by tourists. On one of these visits,

I came away with a rare hardback offering – a novel by a British writer, Reginald Hill, titled *On Beulah Height*. The shop-owner told me in broken English that the book was brand-new and had just arrived in the shop that day, left there by an English cousin. I purchased it and read it over the course of the following days and found its story of a flooded village and the disappearance of three little girls quietly disturbing. Even after I'd finished, the novel left a strange effect on me – like a feeling of dread I couldn't shake off. I lent it to you, and you read it whilst lying on the sand, then later stretched out on your bed in the dorm, your feet brushing against the edge of the frame, your toes occasionally rippling the sheet and pillows. After you finished, I looked up at you, hoping to see the impact the novel had on me etched on your face, but you just shrugged and said, 'It was very readable,' then went off to have a shower. I found the lack of reaction quietly heartbreaking, as if the opinion of a person I'd known for less than two weeks mattered more to me than anyone else's in the world.

For some reason, your reaction to the book bothered me, remaining on my mind long into the night. I felt very small and insecure, lying there awake as you slept peacefully in the bed next to me. I felt as though my soul had been weighed and found wanting next to yours. I knew this was an overreaction – no two people could be expected to always agree about something as subjective as literature. But it bothered me that you hadn't considered how your dismissive reaction would land. You either hadn't read the situation well – hadn't clocked that I was keen to share an experience that had had a notable effect on me. Or, worse still, you *had* clocked it and you didn't care.

I eventually drifted off to sleep, and in my dreams the water was rising. Just as in the book, the streets around me were flooding, and I was trapped in the room, unable to do anything, unable to move out of my bed, unable to stop the crushing destruction that awaited me as the water burst through the door.

Suddenly, there were hands upon me, hands trying to stop me writhing, holding me still, and a voice telling me it was OK, everything was OK, that I was safe. It took me a while to realise that it was your hands on me that I could feel. Your arms wrapped around my shoulders, telling me I was just having a nightmare. You soothed me and I let you, all the while silently begging you not to let me go. In your arms, everything did indeed feel OK. I fell back asleep with you next to me, lying above the covers, but still with your arms on me. Whether you stayed for five minutes or five hours, I couldn't tell, as when I woke up you were damp from the shower, towelling yourself dry on the other side of the room, as if I'd slipped back in time to the first morning we'd properly met.

You didn't refer to my nightmare, didn't ask me what it was about or show any sign of embarrassment. We went out for breakfast as normal and chatted about the sun as the morning heat rose and the birds swooped low along the edges of the shore.

As we approached Saturday, we spoke a little about the plans to go to Argento's island. I could tell you were keen, so I continued to nod along, not wanting to disappoint you. But I still couldn't shake off a nagging feeling – a feeling of something huge, daunting, important, hovering just out of reach. I felt if we crossed the water to this strange man's villa, we'd be out of control. At the mercy of fate. The truth was, I had become so enamoured with our comfortable, companionable routine, I was afraid of anything that might change it. If someone had told me that I could spend the rest of my days enjoying the Greek summer with you, I would have been perfectly content. I had escaped the humdrum, predictable, suffocating existence I felt I had been living and stepped into something that felt fresh and exciting. But I was also aware that if you got restless, you might leave. And that terrified me more than anything else.

On the Friday, I had nipped back to the villa to change my clothes and put in an appearance to reassure my parents I was still very much alive and well. I'd decided this was the best way to remain on their good side, hoping my mother had abandoned her idea of a 'nice family holiday' and got used to my absence. She seemed pleasingly free of any concern when I greeted her by the poolside and was busy sampling a new type of cake-like delicacy Achilles had rustled up for her. 'Oh, hello, Oliver,' she said, barely looking up, as I went inside with the feeling that I need not have bothered.

Upstairs I found Douglas sitting on his bed in something of a mood. He greeted me quite frostily and when I asked what was wrong he got up saying, 'Oh, nothing,' with a sigh.

'Have I pissed you off?' I asked. He laughed and shook his head. 'It's not you. It's just…I had hoped I'd see Nita again. I felt we kind of…well, clicked. She said she'd be sure to "see me around", which I took to mean she would visit again. I've got no way of contacting her – she didn't give me a phone number.

And I think it would be awkward trying to reach her through Dad's friend.'

I nodded, slowly, unsure how to tackle this subject. I was contemplating telling him I would be soon be going somewhere Nita was likely to be, presuming she was still with Argento. But something stopped me. It felt like our secret. Yours and mine. A secret I wasn't ready to share, or to have scrutinised by someone 'on the outside'.

'Do you think I should ask Dad if he has a way of contacting her?' he asked.

'I wouldn't,' I replied, 'Even if she didn't let on to Dad what she does for a living, he's probably guessed.'

Douglas sighed. 'True. And anyway, he's still being…well, weird.'

I nodded and decided to leave the conversation there. I exited the villa and started to make my way back to you, although I couldn't help feeling bad about my caginess. I barely kept any secrets from my brother, but now it felt as though I was working up a steady number, gaining more as the days went on. I'd have to hope I could remember them all.

When I rejoined you later that afternoon, you were keen to visit a beach we had been to briefly once before – a gorgeous, often deserted cove, about a three-mile walk from the centre of town.

'I love it here,' you said, throwing yourself down on the hot sand. You seemed content to sunbathe so I pulled out the dog-eared paperback I was in the middle of and read silently next to you. 'Good book?' you asked when I set it aside. I nodded, but after my experience of you reading *On Beulah Height*, I'd become guarded about sharing my thoughts. If I cared too much about what you thought, I'd run the risk of forgetting to enjoy things myself. I'd learned, growing up, to be careful how much to let on to others about what I cared for, what mattered to me, what I loved and got excited by. The idea of there being an abundance of literature out there waiting to be discovered thrilled me, and when I started to show this, probably aged ten or eleven, I spotted at once the disapproval in my parents. When they saw me reading a book, they implied I was 'being idle'. If I spent the day in the library, or curled up under a tree in the garden, one of them would comment about me 'doing nothing all day'. My mother would hurriedly think up lots of tasks I should be doing, like organising clothes into piles for the local church fundraiser, or my father would ask his brother, my Uncle Frederick (a retired schoolmaster from Eton), to send over some old Latin test papers for me to do at weekends or holidays. All to stop me, I presumed, from having too much fun.

'I'd like to be a writer,' I told you. It was the first time I'd said it out loud, that day on the beach at the empty cove.

'So write,' you said, simply.

I shrugged. 'I don't know. I think I'm still waiting for enough to happen to me before I start.'

You frowned. 'Enough of what?'

I laughed, realising I didn't have specifics to hand. 'Life, I guess.'

I looked at you, wondering if you had any more to say. You'd started to unwrap the breads we'd bought on the way and handed me some. They were still fresh and delicious, and I posted crusty mouthfuls into my mouth as I stared out to sea.

'I've been thinking about what you said.' You spoke quietly as you pulled yourself up on your hands, leaning forward so we could see each other.

'What did I say?'

'About not having lived enough yet. And, well, I think we shouldn't be afraid to be more daring about things. Say yes to experiences we wouldn't otherwise say yes to.'

I felt a leap in my stomach and edged closer towards you. 'Such as?'

'Such as going to the island tomorrow.'

I didn't say anything. Even then, I think I felt like I was being manoeuvred, although I didn't know why or to what extent. But I was still hesitant to be too bold, to be a voice of dissent.

I don't know how long the silence lasted, but eventually you picked up the book I had set down.

'*The Pale King*', you said, running a finger over the title. You flicked through it then asked, 'Are these short stories?'

'Sort of,' I said, '*The Pale King* is a play within the book that…well, it dooms people who see it or read it.'

'Dooms?' you asked, the yellow of the cover reflecting on the underside of your chin, giving your tanned skin a gorgeous glow. 'In what way?'

'Madness,' I said. 'It sends them mad. They're never the same again.'

I turned my gaze out to sea and noticed that one of the sailing boats that had been going by now and then seemed to have come to a stop. Whether it had moored on a buoy or dropped its anchor, I didn't know. But I could just about make out a figure, standing on it. Watching us.

'I think we're being observed,' I said, raising a hand to point.

You leaned forward and squinted into the distance. 'I think it's a man, but that's all I can see. Just seems to be standing there.'

'Watching,' I said, feeling a prickle of unease.

You laughed. 'Perhaps it's The Pale King.'

You meant it lightly, I was sure, but since I had just experienced that strange and disturbing book, your comment didn't make me feel any better.

'Or Argento,' I said, giving up trying to make out the figure and lying back down.

'It could be anyone,' you said, picking up the book again. 'Right, you've intrigued me, I'm going to read some of this. You can lie there and look beautiful.'

Chapter Eleven

THEN

The next day we arrived on the jetty by Marco's Bar, ready to go to Argento's island. We hadn't spoken about it much leading up to that moment. As soon as it became clear that you seemed to think it was something we should be saying yes to, I was happy to go along with the plan. Our moments of intimacy, infrequent and relatively fleeting as they both had been, had plunged me into a new way of living – a new terrain that was ruled by your whims and desires, and I was your grateful, adoring servant. I didn't even mind. To say I found everything about you intoxicating would be like saying the sun was bright. It wasn't just your beauty, although I'm certain that was a large part of it. It was the way you looked at me, the way you touched me, and the way that you never quite let me get below the surface. I never quite knew what you were thinking, deep down. And that made me want you even more.

The boat that came to collect us was staffed by an old man who didn't seem to speak much English, and I lacked enough

Greek to really make out what he was saying as he murmured and pointed at things whilst steering out to sea towards one of the nearby islands. I noticed you watching me at one point. 'What?' I asked, laughing a little as I said it.

'Nothing,' you said, 'I'm just taking you in, Oliver Churchfield. Just taking you all in.'

As the boat navigated the rocky cliffs that surrounded the island, a wooden dock area came into sight. I could see the figure of a man standing, waiting for our arrival. He was dressed in a beige shirt featuring delicately embroidered patterns, and dark green trousers. The style didn't look particularly Greek, or English, and I wondered if it was something Argento had picked up on his travels. I wondered, too, what other parts of the world this man had been to, and what strange adventures he must have had while there. I still didn't understand why he had invited us, exactly, or what would be expected of us. As I stepped off the boat, I felt a sense of disquiet and wondered if I had been wise not to tell my father about this secret assignation involving a would-be business contact of his.

'Gentlemen,' Argento said, his hands open in greeting. 'Welcome to Cruciamen Island. My home when I am not elsewhere.'

'Thank you for inviting us,' I said, slightly unsure whether we should be shaking his hand or embracing or just standing awkwardly. We chose the latter – or at least I did. I noticed you looked relaxed, just standing there, your usual half-smile on your lips, your sandy-blonde hair fluttering in the early-evening breeze.

'Please come this way,' he said and led us through a gap in the tall plants up a row of steps to a grand-looking villa.

'Your villa is…impressive,' I said, as it came into view properly.

'It's called Villa Tassos,' he said. 'I hope you will both enjoy your time here. Please do make yourselves comfortable.'

I felt his words were a strange choice, considering we were only supposed to be there for that evening. It sounded like he was welcoming us to stay for longer.

As we climbed, we reached what appeared to be the entrance of the villa. Its stone walls at the front held two burning torches, and although the sun had not yet set, they cast a warm glow around us that made the outside light seem darker than it was, as if we'd journeyed into the night as we'd climbed the steps.

Argento led us through the grand entrance without saying a word and we walked in companionable silence, our footsteps echoing on the tiled floor. The villa had a long, wide corridor and high ceilings, which made it feel even more grand. The design was more ornate and intricate than the modern and comparatively unimaginative villa my family owned. The main walkway through the building had corridors branching off on each side, but we didn't go down any of these, just carried on straight through until we came out into an open area, still covered, but very much part of the outside world, with impressive pillars and a large stone veranda that surrounded a swimming pool in its centre.

'I like it here,' you said, smiling, turning to look at me. I nodded – I agreed that it was impressive, and I'd already said as much. But I was more struck by the swimming pool, or rather the person in it. I don't think you'd noticed, but I'd clocked that we were not alone. The young woman swam to the shallow entry steps and started to climb out. I saw your gaze turn to her. Your smile remained, though I noticed your eyes widen as she approached us, completely naked. It was Nita. She walked slowly over to us, dripping all the way, the water leaving dark patches that gleamed on the floor in the light of the warm-toned lamps that hung from the pillars.

'It's a pleasure to see you again, Oliver,' she said in her smooth American accent.

'This is Oliver's friend, Alastair,' Argento said, nodding at you. You stepped forward and took Nita's hand.

'Charmed,' you said. She took your hand, a slanted, almost knowing smile on her mouth.

'Why don't you join me in the pool?' She laid a hand on my arm, as if to pull me towards the steps. I smiled politely, but took a step back.

'We don't have our swimming things,' I said.

Nita gave a very slight shrug. 'I don't mind. Come in anyway, wearing all your clothes. Or none of them.' She stared me in the eye, the challenge evident, but I just laughed again and diverted my gaze to the floor. As I did so, I thought I heard you sigh a little. Perhaps the thought of skinny-dipping in this private pool excited you. Perhaps you were disappointed I hadn't jumped at the invitation. Though I may have been imagining it, I couldn't help feeling like I'd failed a test in some way.

'Nita,' Argento said, appearing to my left. I had almost

forgotten he was with us. 'Perhaps you would like to stop tormenting our guests and dry yourself. It is nearly time for dinner to be served.'

Still with a lingering smile playing about her lips, Nita walked away from us to where a pile of towels sat on a glass table and began to wrap one round herself.

'She has a bold spirit within her,' Argento said. 'I told her we would be having two interesting young men for dinner. She rarely has such vivacious company to look forward to.'

He led us around the pool, weaving his way through the towering pillars and towards a large table on a terrace surrounded by colourful plants and luscious trees. I paused. Argento's wording had, rather unsettlingly, made it sound as if we weren't just the guests. We were the meal as well.

Chapter Twelve

THEN

O ur dinner wasn't dissimilar to the lunch we had had earlier that week and consisted of me feeling ill at ease whilst you effortlessly made small talk and participated in our host's conversations. There were times, after long periods of silence on my part, when I would allow my gaze to wander, only to find Argento's eyes staring right into mine. When this happened, I would smile and busy myself selecting some more of the cured meats and cheeses on offer in front of us, all the while feeling the intensity of his gaze. I focused instead on what Nita was saying, as she spoke candidly about her life back in the US, at boarding school when she was a teenager, and how after high school she found herself working for a touring illusionist in the American Midwest.

'What was that like?' I heard you ask.

'He was a cruel man,' Nita said, 'I don't miss those days. His illusions were big, outlandish, made the audience gasp. He played with the boundaries between magic and reality.

Conjured things people hadn't seen before, or hadn't ever dared to imagine. All tricks, you understand, but extremely well done. He filled both local town halls and grand arenas. But he expected me to pleasure his grown-up sons, who travelled with us and worked alongside him. I did as I was asked, I didn't want to cause any hassle, I relied on the money. I found pleasure in it, at times. But if I wasn't successful in pleasing them, he would withhold food from me. It was a difficult time.'

This was such a disturbing testimony of her past employment, I expected some reaction from Argento – at least a look of sombre respect or a shake of the head. But he continued to sit there, smiling at us pleasantly, as if nothing about Nita's story concerned him. Part of me wondered if this was all part of Nita's role as his paid companion. I once again had that sense of artificiality I'd experienced during her visit with the fruit basket: the feeling that I was in the audience at a play, and that what we were witnessing was, in fact, a performance – not honest biography but a story scripted for her by her employer for our – what? Amusement? Entertainment? I couldn't think why Argento or Nita would do such a thing, but the more I continued to listen, the more unsettled I became.

'That wasn't the only thing he did,' Nita continued. 'He was strange about food. Told all of us who travelled with him that food was scarce, but then would set up a banquet for himself that he'd eat throughout the day, feasting on it, like he was desperate for it. He wasn't overweight, but he was a large man, very tall, with muscles. Such muscles. So he'd eat to keep them firm, keep up his shape. Then he'd invite the rest of us to select some of the scraps. Some of the performers in his show or technical team could afford to go out to the town to get their own food, but he'd put obstacles in their way. Always find a reason they weren't allowed to find shops or a café. Or he'd blackmail or threaten the workers at the restaurants, saying if they served his staff they would wake up with their legs broken or find powdered glass in their mouths. There were times when we even had to take food left behind by the audiences who came to watch his shows. He knew how to control people with hunger, you see.' She looked down at the table, the food on her plate, then said, 'I guess this is not the right time for such a story.'

It was a bit late now, I thought, as images of a desperately hungry circus troupe came into my mind, standing huddled under show lights as an audience threw crusts of bread at them.

I didn't know what I'd expected when we'd arrived at the island, but after the food had been eaten, Argento stood and said it was time for us to depart. It was an abrupt ending and I couldn't help feeling an odd sense of anticlimax as we said goodbye to Nita, who remained at the table, running her hands through her golden hair, as if preoccupied with other thoughts. As I stood to go, however, she spoke again, looking straight at me. 'Do say hello to your brother. He was very nice to me the other day. I'd love to see him again, if he too was free to visit.' I just nodded and said I'd ask him.

When we got to the wooden dock where the boat was moored and waiting, you thanked Argento and climbed aboard. I was about to do the same, when he said something that made me freeze.

'I have a message for your father.'

I turned around and looked at him. I noticed you had stopped too. Nobody said anything for a long moment.

'My...my father?' I asked. It took me by surprise, momentarily forgetting the connection he had to him.

'Yes,' Argento said, 'please could you tell him that I'm waiting.'

I opened my mouth, then paused, sure there must be something more to it than that. When Argento didn't continue, I asked 'Just that?'

He gave a single nod. 'Just that.'

'I'll...I'll tell him,' I said, wishing I had been given a less ambiguous message. Then something crossed my mind.

'Should I mention this place?' I wasn't sure why I was asking permission. Perhaps because I hadn't involved my family in my plans, it had become a secret – a secret I should continue keeping.

'That is up to you,' he said. 'If it makes things easier, you can tell him we met on the seafront outside a café by chance. That is, after all, the truth, is it not?' He smiled, then took a step closer and said, 'It was nice to see people using that cove. It remains empty for much of the summer. I often go there to meditate and I was pleased to see you and Alastair there.'

I felt a blush start to spread over my face, and felt embarrassed, 'You...you saw us...'

'Oh, I see everything that happens around here. I'm always watching, you see. Promise me you'll come back and visit next weekend. Same arrangement. And bring your brother, too. It seems Nita has been quite taken with him. And she deserves a few more amusements before her time on this island comes to an end. For we all must enjoy what we have while it lasts. Make sure you both remember that.' He nodded at me, then looked over to you, already on the boat, waiting to leave.

I wasn't sure what else to say, so chose not to speak. I just nodded back and stepped into the boat, my mind in a spin.

Chapter Thirteen

THEN

We didn't speak on the boat ride back. The old man didn't try to make conversation apart from once, when he pointed at the sea, where the water appeared to be moving strangely – bubbling almost – and started to say something in Greek that I didn't understand. Eventually, he just said, 'Fish. Lots.' I nodded, barely registering any interest.

After our time on the island, it felt as if our relationship had been stepped up in some way. It was almost as if Argento's words had given us permission to carry on this adventure we were on. This adventure with each other.

I wondered if I should go back to the family villa straightaway, to pass on Argento's message to my father. But that was an experience I decided was best tackled in daylight, if I chose to go through with it at all. I was still uneasy about him knowing I was attending meals hosted by his business acquaintances without him knowing.

So I followed you back to the quiet darkness of your hostel. You kissed me as I was about to take off my shirt. You helped me do it, unbuttoning it, firmly but not roughly, and setting it aside before kissing me again. I kissed you back. Everything was slow at first. Like the night was taking in a deep, long breath. Then the sudden exhale – the two of us drawing apart, rushing to get the rest of our clothes off, falling back onto your bed, together, as one.

Afterwards, all I could hear was the sound of the waves from beyond the window and the beating of our hearts. We lay on our backs, my arm over your shoulder. My mind seemed to have divided into two streams. One was full of questions. Were we headed for a full-on relationship? Would you become my boyfriend? Or was this a summer fling for you? Would you discard me once the novelty had worn off? At the same time, the other stream of thinking was pure bliss. A bliss that loved the feeling of your hand resting somewhere above my left knee. The feeling of your hair brushing against my wrist as you lay, relaxed in my embrace. The feeling that we might be able to do that all over again very soon.

As if you could read my thoughts, you turned over so you could see me properly. 'I want to do this with you for ever,' I said. 'Every day, every moment, every second of my life.' I didn't care how intense it sounded, how presumptuous it might seem. You didn't seem alarmed, but didn't say anything – just kissed me deeply, then gently pulled away, smiling at me as you did so, brushing my cheek with the palm of your hand. 'Will your family be missing you?'

I looked up, taken aback. You had rarely asked about my family, and I'd got the feeling you didn't have much interest in my life outside of us. Perhaps you had heard the message Argento had asked me to pass on, I thought. 'No. Well, they might. But as we've already established, I'm an adult,' I said, playfully kissing his shoulder, 'capable of making adult decisions.' I kissed your neck, then up to your cheek.

'It was touch and go whether I'd even make it to Greece,' I said. 'I overslept the morning we were coming here. Almost missed the flight. My dad and I had a disagreement the night before. I had some old school friends over for a few drinks and it turned into more of a party than a gathering.'

'You don't seem like the partying type,' you said.

I didn't know whether to be offended by this or not. But it was a fair comment, I decided. 'Yeah, well…I'd just returned from uni and was keen to make sure this summer didn't become…I don't know…just like any of the other summers. It was a while since I'd seen everyone, so I tried to liven things up. But I'm pleased I wasn't left behind. I'm pleased I got on the plane.'

You met my eye. Smiled that small, bewitching smile that never failed to quicken my heart rate. 'I'm pleased too,' you said.

Much as I wanted to spend the next day with you, I decided I should spend some time at the villa with my family. When I let myself in, I could hear Dad having a heated phone call in one of the downstairs rooms, the door closed. I made my way through the large glass doors at the back of the villa to find my mother lounging by the pool, as usual, flicking through one of her magazines, an irritated look on her face.

'I'm back,' I said, then immediately regretted my choice of

words, in case they placed too much emphasis on the fact I had been gone.

'Nice of you to bother,' my mother said with a sniff.

'Come on, don't be like that,' I said with a sigh, letting myself drop into one of the sun loungers next to her. The gentle sound of the trees swaying in the breeze could have sent me right back off to sleep. But my mother's voice cut through the tranquillity.

'What did you *think* we'd be like? I think we're very understanding, very…very…*modern* with you and your activities and believe me when I say it, it's taken some convincing behind the scenes to bring your father on board. But there is a limit, you know.'

'Sorry, what?' I asked, confused.

'Your father saw you. You were on the beach meeting a man…*kissing* him. Brazenly, in daylight.'

Even though part of me was rather mortified to learn this, I couldn't help but half-laugh, half-splutter in indignation at my mother's words.

'*Brazenly*? Mum, you do know this is 1997, not 1957.'

She closed her magazine with as much of a snap as its flimsy pages would allow. 'We are *abroad*,' she hissed. 'This isn't *England*, this is…' She trailed off as Achilles wandered into view, setting a plate of small cakes down on the wicker table next to my mother. 'For your enjoyment,' he smiled, then walked off.

I looked down at the cakes. 'Does he just do this all day, everyday?' I asked.

'That's what he's paid to do,' she said, still sounding cross, reaching for a cake.

'And you don't worry about…I don't know…becoming diabetic.'

I knew I'd said the wrong thing as soon as my mother's eyes flared. Health concerns were one of her 'things' and it was enough to make her drop the cake on the plate and hurriedly swallow the mouthful she'd taken. 'What a *horrible* thing to say! Are you suggesting I'm overeating? That I'm *overweight*?'

'Well, no, you're not—'

'I can't believe you'd be so…so…'

'What's going on?' My father's voice echoed from the doorway behind us.

'Oliver was just telling me how I'm…I'm…*ballooning*.'

'I didn't say anything of the—'

'It certainly sounded like that to me.'

Dad frowned. 'Why would you say that to your mother, Oliver?'

I stood up, outraged, 'You're believing her?' I looked around, but there was nobody to back me up. 'Where's Douglas?' I asked, suddenly noticing his absence.

'Swimming,' Mum said. 'Alone, because you've abandoned him. And don't change the subject.'

'I haven't abandoned him,' I said, regretting my decision to come back at all, wishing I'd just spent the day away.

'Well, I rather think you have,' my father said, folding his arms. 'We don't know what's going on with you, lately. Never know where you are, who you're…spending time with.'

'He's going off the rails,' my mother said, reaching again for a cake, apparently the fear of limb amputation now a distant memory, 'It happened to Timmy Baythorne's son. He found him with drugs. Prostitutes and drugs.'

'I haven't been taking drugs, or mixing with prostitutes,' I snapped back, then something occurred to me. 'In fact, if you're worried about the latter, you should talk to your other son.'

'What does that mean?' My father frowned.

I'd planned on picking my words carefully around this subject, but I'd become so riled up that any sense of caution had gone out the window. 'Well, Douglas is the one lusting after that Nita your business friend is paying. She's an escort, didn't you know? Oh, and Argento has a message for you. He says he's *waiting*, whatever the fuck that means.'

I turn to go.

'Steady on there,' Dad called out to me. 'What do you mean he's waiting? How do you...who...where did you...'

He trailed off. I paused trying to steady my breath and calm myself down. 'I just...bumped into him,' I said, flatly.

'When?' Dad barked, his face growing pale.

'Last night. Near...near the sea.'

It wasn't entirely a lie, although far from the whole story, and I think my father could tell I wasn't being entirely forthcoming. He stared at me for a few seconds, then nodded. 'Very well. I'll see to it.'

He blustered off, back into the villa.

'You've upset him,' my mother said, tutting.

'Well, that makes a change,' I muttered back, and went inside, planning to sulk in my room.

It was later that evening when the phone call came. I'd mooched about most of the day, picking up books and putting them down again, trying to keep to my room as much as possible. When I went downstairs, feeling hungry, I saw that Dad was trying to get the barbecue going, with Achilles standing patiently next to him holding a tray of meat ready to be cooked.

As I was on my way I heard a ringing coming from the living room. I looked inside to see my father's mobile on the coffee table. I picked it up, answered and said, 'Hi, sorry, can you hold for a sec.' I went back out to the corridor and called out 'Dad! Phone!', but he didn't hear, so I shouted 'Dad!' again, going to the doorway.

'What?' he yelled back. 'Just wait a moment!'

Fuck it, I thought, turning away, putting the phone to my ear. 'He's not available,' I said bluntly. 'You'll need to call back.' I was about to cut the call when the person at the other end spoke.

'No problem, tell him John called,' a man's voice said. 'John Foal-Amos.' Then the line went dead.

I chucked the phone onto one of the chairs in the living room, then made my way outside for the evening, gearing up for battle once more.

Chapter Fourteen

THEN

I returned to your hostel each night for the week that followed, and I kept my visits back to my family's villa infrequent and brief. Often I'd miss Douglas, who would be out when I was there, having taken himself off on a hike, while Mum and Dad seemed unable to decide whether to moan at me or ignore me altogether. I'd begun to feel guilty at how little I'd seen my brother over the past week, and woke up on Wednesday morning with the aim of going to find him and apologise, perhaps even confide in him properly and fill him in on everything that had been happening. Any need to hunt for him – or even to return home – vanished, however, when the door to the dorm room opened and in he walked.

'Well, this is an interesting sight,' he said, hands on his hips.

I rubbed my eyes, a beam of morning sun causing me to blink and crane my head forward, although I knew the voice. I just couldn't believe what I was hearing.

'Douglas? What the fuck?'

'So this is where you've been enjoying yourself.' He nodded towards you. 'Who's this, then?'

By some miracle you remained asleep.

'What? Oh…we shouldn't wake him,' I said, lowering my voice. 'He was up late.'

'Was he now,' Douglas said, copying my low volume, giving me a sly smile and sitting down on the mattress opposite. 'You two do look rather cosy on that single. Please don't tell me you're renting a bed here? I know Mum and Dad are bad but this is extreme.'

'No, I'm not,' I said, still keeping my voice low. 'Look… how did you get in here? How did you know where I was?'

'In answer to your first question,' Douglas said, 'the lovely young lady downstairs said I could go up and take a look at the size of the beds. I said, being a tall guy, I needed to make sure my feet wouldn't be hanging off the end. She seemed to find this quite funny. Very relaxed. I think she finds her job boring.'

'Well, she's barely batted an eyelid at me coming or going,' I conceded. 'But I don't get how—'

'Followed you,' he said with a shrug. 'Saw you and pretty boy here heading in here when I was out for a late-night stroll last night. Decided to pay you a morning visit.'

'I'm honoured,' I said with a sigh.

I felt you starting to stir next to me. 'What's happening?' you mumbled, your eyes slowly blinking open.

'Hey, I'm your bed-buddy's older brother,' Douglas said, offering his hand.

You shook it, looking confused and still half asleep, rubbing your eyes.

'Douglas, maybe we could catch up later?' I said, looking at him, hoping he'd notice how embarrassing I found this situation and retreat now that you were awake.

'I think I'll take a shower while you two talk,' you said, getting out of bed and straightening up. 'I'll be back in a bit.' I watched as you grabbed your towel, tied it round your waist and headed out.

'So what's going on here?' Douglas said, as soon as your footsteps had died away. 'Quick work, eh? Already shacked up with some—'

'We're not *shacked up*. It's all happened very...I don't know...'

'Are we talking summer fling or summer romance?' Douglas said, the sly smile still on his lips.

'It's just some...summer fun,' I said. I didn't know why I was trying to diminish what I felt for you and how strong my feelings were. Douglas's sudden gate-crashing made me seem like my time with you was under threat – like the outside world was threatening to break into our sun-soaked, dreamlike existence. I usually welcomed my brother's company, but for the first time in my life I felt like he was more irritant than welcome presence. And it annoyed me all the more that he didn't seem to realise that.

'Well, leaving your holiday fling aside, I'm tempted to do what you've almost done and get a bed here.'

I frowned at him. 'You're not serious?'

Douglas groaned, 'I had a major row with Dad last night. He was being unnecessarily unkind to Mum and I told him he was a prick. It was sort of a final-straw situation. It's why I left for a walk, needed time away from them.'

I nodded. I understood how he felt. 'Well, don't make any sudden decisions. See how things are.'

He raised an eyebrow, 'Worried I'll disturb your little love nest? Don't worry. I'm not here to stop your *summer fun*. By the way, I'm starving – I didn't eat last night because of the row. Shall we go out for breakfast?'

I got out of bed and started to get dressed, 'Err, yes, well, I suppose so.'

'Your guy can come too,' Douglas said. I knew he was attempting to be nice, showing me I had nothing to worry about when it came to welcoming a potential romantic interest of mine. But I felt like I'd been cornered, thrown into a particularly awkward situation, and wasn't in the right frame of mind to feel anything as generous as gratitude.

'His name is Alastair,' I said, stuffing my feet into my shoes. The door swung open and in you walked.

'Talk of the devil,' Douglas said. 'We were thinking of getting breakfast. Want to come?'

As your eyes met mine, I had to stop myself from drawing in a breath, feeling my chest swell as it often did when I looked at you.

'Breakfast sounds lovely,' you said, then flashed a smile at Douglas. 'I'd like to get to know Oliver's brother.'

'Splendid,' Douglas said, getting up. 'I'll meet you downstairs, let you get dressed. Wouldn't mind another chat with that charming girl on the desk.' He winked at me and laughed.

Our late-morning breakfast was, on the whole, relaxed and enjoyable, the warmth of the sun already strong on our backs as we ate outside overlooking the sea, watching a group of young men rush into the waves, laughing and whooping, and further down two young American kids with their parents being told off for refusing to apply suncream. Only one moment concerned me a little. Whilst you were talking, giving Douglas a little summary of your family history and why you were travelling, I watched you speak until you'd finished your story. Afterwards, I glanced away and caught Douglas looking at me, his eyes narrowed a little. I realised I'd been smiling the whole time I was listening to you, and wondered if Douglas had twigged that our pairing wasn't the casual holiday fling I'd made out. Perhaps, I thought to myself, infatuation was the most impossible thing to hide – especially from those who knew you well.

Chapter Fifteen

NOW

'You knew how I felt about you,' I say, sitting beside you for the first time in years. 'How could you not tell me you were alive?'

You turn to look at me. 'There are so many questions I need to ask you too. I imagine you know what they are. There are things...things I'd like to know about how...how you could have done it. Even if you felt betrayed. By some of the choices I made. Some of the...mistakes. If you loved me. How was it even possible to do what you did?'

I stay silent.

'Of course, I know it's possible to betray someone you love,' you continue.

'I don't want to talk about what you did,' I say.

'I understand that. I've had a long time to think about it. But in terms of your choice – what *you* did – I suppose that isn't about *capability*, is it? It's about reasoning. And I'd like to hear it from you.'

I try to steady my breathing. 'You first,' I say, quietly.

You take a breath, but then I hear the crunch and rustle of someone approaching; then, from the side of the bench, in the direction of the greater grounds, a woman appears. The same woman I fell over in front of earlier. The one who kept wanting to chat to me at breakfast.

'Oh, hello,' she says, offering a small smile. Her eyes flicker over to you. 'Who's this?' she asks.

'A friend,' I reply, hopefully with a sense of finality to it. I don't mean to be unfriendly, but I just kind of want her to – well – fuck off. But she is either oblivious to my rudeness or chooses to ignore it.

'It must be nice to have a friend,' she says, turning to look over at the lawn. 'I don't really have any. Here or…out there…'

She doesn't say anything for a few moments. 'Right,' I say, resisting the urge to shriek at her. *She doesn't know*, I tell myself, *Be kind to her, she doesn't know what she's interrupting. She's just lonely.* So both of us sit in silence, while she lingers, then she says: 'I was going to go and get a hot chocolate from the machine inside. Would either of you two…'

'We're fine, thank you,' you say, your tone more gentle than mine had been. I see you smile. Still got the old charm, I notice. That quiet, irresistible smile that makes me want to feel your arms around me again.

'OK, well…I'll leave you both to your *deep chats*,' she says, emphasising the last two words playfully. Then she walks away.

You raise an eyebrow at me. 'Who is she?'

I shrug. 'No idea. I think she just wants someone to talk to. Share things with. Go through all this together, whatever her "this" is. I haven't yet worked that out. Drugs, maybe.'

You shake your head. 'I reckon it's more of a psychological than a physical addiction. Grief, perhaps. Or trauma.'

'Aren't all addictions both psychological and physical in some way?'

You sigh. 'We can talk about your own addiction if you want to. I presume that's why you're here? You have a…well, a problem. What is it you do with your life? Are you missing work to be here?'

I feel my hands clench. 'I don't want to talk about it.'

'Are you sure?'

I reach round and start rubbing my back, imagining a sudden pain there. Feeling like I need it to stop, otherwise it might carry on for ever and ever, torturing me.

'I think you should,' you say.

'And I'm telling you I don't want to,' I reply. 'Really.'

'There was a time when you'd have told me anything. Everything.' You don't say it in a way that suggests you want any conflict. But I do feel like you're deliberately trying to press me. Trying to needle me a little, perhaps. And it annoys me. Especially when I consider, for a moment, that you might have a point. You might have a valid reason to want to cause me discomfort. Presuming you know everything about what happened that night in Greece.

'I don't want to talk about my addiction.'

'Your work then. Tell me what you ended up doing. Did your love of books and reading lead where you always dreamed? Did you start writing?'

'No.' I feel a twinge in my throat as I say it. 'I'm an accountant.'

You don't have to tell me what you think of this. I can hear it in your silence. The weight of my crushed dreams and disappointment echoing between us. It becomes more than I can bear, so eventually I say, 'I've struggled with addiction to painkillers but now I'm getting better. That's all you need to know.'

You sit in silence for a few moments, then you nod. 'OK. That's fair enough. And I suppose it's only natural.'

You're doing it again. Teasing me, saying things that will lead to further questions. And I didn't have much option but to go along with it.

'Why is it only natural?'

I'm not looking at you but I can hear the smile in your voice.

'Well, your addiction to me. And to other things. Things that happened on the island.'

I don't want to go there. I've spent so much of my life not unpacking those thoughts – or trying to unpack them within a safe space, paying therapists a fortune whilst never truly saying out loud what I had done. What had happened on the island and how everything started. My experiences keeping me prisoner.

As I raise my hand to touch my back and shoulder again, I can feel it shaking. 'I'm not sure I can do this.'

'I thought you wanted to know,' you say, your tone hard to interpret. 'I thought you wanted to know why I'm alive.'

'And why I'm only just hearing about it.'

I hear you take in a long breath. 'It was actually out of respect. Respect for you. For your family. I didn't want a scandal, didn't want anything coming out that could make things awkward.'

'*Awkward*?' I could have laughed if I hadn't already been so tense.

'Well, difficult, then.'

Difficult. I let the word sit between us. Yes, this was difficult.

'Even in the early days, I could sense you were falling too hard for me. Too hard…becoming too dependent.'

'Too *dependent*?'

You sigh. 'It was too much. Things were…I don't know… burning so bright. Soon they were going to burn out, one way or another. So when they did, when…when an easy exit was provided, I took it.'

I don't say anything. What you say next, though, does surprise me.

'Believe me when I say this, Oliver: the years of silence, years of…nothing…I did that out of kindness. Truly.'

'Kindness?' I repeat, the word sounding strange and foreign in my mouth.

'Yes. Kindness.'

I find it hard to believe or comprehend what he is telling me. I take a deep breath, then start to speak. 'I wish I hadn't been so blind. Blinded by my attraction to you, my need to be near you. Until you betrayed me, of course. Then my eyes were opened.'

Chapter Sixteen

THEN

Once I'd got used to Douglas and you being around at the same time, things ended up working rather well. Although he was a little too 'present' at times, causing me to self-censor how affectionate I was with you (the idea of kissing you with him in the nearby vicinity mortified me), it was nevertheless a more relaxing set-up than I would have expected.

Things all seemed to be going smoothly until the day we were set for our second visit to Argento's island, when Douglas dropped something of a bombshell. I had spent the night in your hostel dorm, as had become my default. Douglas, who hadn't followed through on his threat to rent a room there, walked down from the family villa early in the morning. He'd planned to meet us, but had arrived an hour early, while we were still in bed.

'Oliver!' he called from the door, 'I need to talk.'

'Christ,' I grumbled as I rolled round, the pillows

surprisingly cool on my cheeks considering the heat of the room. 'It's early, Doug,' I called back.

Without further warning the door opened and I heard footsteps enter the room.

'Jesus, can't this wait,' I said, closing my eyes and burying my head in the pillow.

'No, it can't.' He sat down on the bed opposite, 'I've had enough. Had enough of both of them.'

'Both of them being…'

'Mum and Dad, obviously,' he snapped.

'What's the problem?' you asked, waking up next to me.

'Doug,' I said, feeling annoyed and embarrassed, 'This is becoming an unfortunate habit of yours, disturbing our mornings and marching in here.'

'I'm serious, Oliver,' he said, ignoring my protests, 'I've decided to leave.'

This got my attention. 'What? Leave Greece?'

'Yes. Last night was just awful. It's all right for you, free-loading it here. I thought about paying for a bed somewhere myself but I've decided it will just be better to cut and run. I need to get going on looking for a new place in London anyway.'

And a job perhaps, I thought, but didn't say it. 'Don't leave. I'm sure it's not all that bad.'

He shook his head. 'I've decided. I'm going to tell them tonight and leave tomorrow. Will you come with me?'

I stared back at him. 'With you? To England?'

'Well, no – but yes, if you wanted to. But I meant will you come back for dinner tonight and back me up with Mum and

Dad? I could do with you there, even if it's to just dilute the fallout.'

'I...suppose,' I said, rubbing my face, feeling exhausted already. I knew how it would play out. Dad would rage that Douglas was ungrateful and Mum would cry and possibly even blame me.

I felt your hand on my shoulder. 'Don't forget, Oliver, we have a commitment this evening.'

I turned to look at you, puzzled. Then realised what you meant. Of course. In all the fuss with Douglas, I'd momentarily forgotten what day it was.

'Commitment? What commitment?' Douglas asked.

'We're...having dinner.' I felt awkward about him still being in the dark about our contact with Argento and Nita, although it seemed inevitable it was all going to come out now.

'You should come with us,' you said.

I thought back to our departure last time. The request that I should bring my brother along next time. A request I had planned on ignoring. But then again, I thought, remembering the unclothed Nita and Douglas's initial interest in her when she'd visited, this could be a way of delaying his rash decision to leave Greece. Plus I thought it might also avoid an unpleasant showdown with our parents.

So I said the words – the words I knew he wouldn't be able to resist as soon as they were uttered.

'Yes, you should come. Nita will be there.'

We went to the beach, sat on the sand, and filled Douglas in on the island and why I'd kept it a secret. I could tell he was put out that I'd left him to endure our parents at the villa while I swanned off on exotic adventures. But I could also tell he understood. And he certainly seemed grateful and excited by the prospect of seeing Nita again.

When evening came and the sun's heat began to dim, we went down to the harbour as planned. The boat arrived and stopped to let us board. Argento met us at the jetty when we arrived at the island. He smiled. 'So now there's three of you. I'm pleased you could come, Douglas. Nita will be delighted.'

Chapter Seventeen

THEN

W e spent the afternoon being shown around the garden on the island, on lower levels than the villa. The whole place seemed to be tiered, so that it was hard to tell sometimes when we were above the surrounding water or about to turn a corner on one of the gravel paths and step into the sea.

'This place is incredible,' Douglas said, just before we turned a corner and came across Nita sunbathing – and, as before, she was completely naked. My eyes flicked to Douglas and I was amused to see him both stunned and delighted.

'What were you saying, Douglas?' I asked, teasingly, suddenly feeling more charitable towards him than I had done for a while.

'Incredible. I mean, this place…incredible,' he muttered, sounding suddenly nervous.

Argento smiled as Nita rose from the sun lounger and walked over, confident as before. She zeroed in on Douglas and touched his shoulder.

'It's nice to see you again,' she said quietly, although we could all hear every word. Every syllable. It was as if the sounds of the trees and surge of the nearby sea had been muted, and all we could hear was her voice. And the sound of Douglas's heart beating as she laid a hand on his chest.

'Nervous?' she asked.

A few seconds' silence passed. Then Douglas asked, 'For what?'

Nita didn't reply. She just smiled and then turned back to return to her lounger.

'Don't play with your food, my darling,' Argento said, with a soft laugh. He then turned to us. 'Come, there is another guest I would like you to meet.'

We dined once again on the stone veranda. The other guest was both surprising and disconcerting. His name was Jax Wolf, and Argento had introduced him as a 'business acquaintance'. He was a young-ish man, with something harsh and rough about his manner and delivery that made him feel ill-matched to our beautiful surroundings.

'I've been in business since I was fourteen,' he said, his East London accent loud and strong. He knocked back a glass of wine before helping himself to a second from the bottle on the table. 'Me and my uncle – he had a business already, but I had the brains. And I tell you what's at the heart of business: fucking brains.' He tapped his head as he said it, in case we weren't sure what he meant, the gesture sending drops of wine spilling onto the collar of his white shirt.

'What sort of business do you do?' asked Douglas, clearly trying to look friendly and interested.

'This and that,' he said with a laugh, then looked over at Argento and, quite unmistakably, winked. 'Spend a lot of my time in South America, Mexico, all around. See the fucking world, I do. See the sights, bed the babes, do all right.' He looked over at Nita, raising his eyebrows a little suggestively. She stared back at him blankly. I saw Douglas's expression grow more hostile and he turned his eyes back to the table.

'So how do you lot all know each other then?' Jax said, grabbing a roll from the bread basket in the table's centre and tearing a chunk off. He proceeded to chew it with his mouth open, staring from me to Douglas, then to you. I wasn't sure what you'd tell him if given the opportunity, so I decided to take command of the situation before anyone else could.

'We're all just friends.'

'*Just* friends?' Jax said, frowning, 'Friends aren't *just* friends, they're the most important fucking people in the whole fucking world. When everything's going to pot and your luck's run out and you think you're going to die, it's friends who pull you out of the pit of hell, I'll tell you that for free.' He used his crust of bread to gesture to me authoritatively. I realised at that moment I really disliked him and wondered why Argento was ruining our dinner by subjecting us to this unwelcome guest's company.

'Well, let us hope your luck hasn't run out,' Argento said in his quiet, low voice.

I suddenly felt quite hot and wanted to rub my forehead, but didn't want to be the first person to move. It was Nita who spoke first after Argento, seemingly unfazed by the awkwardness, puffing on a sweet-smelling cigarette. 'If I could die anywhere, it would certainly be here.'

A strange thing happened not long after that. We had finished eating and Jax had just started on yet another glass of wine when he suddenly gave a noticeable (and, in my view, rather rude) yawn. 'Christ, I feel fucking wrecked,' he said.

'Would you like to lie down?' Argento asked, not moving.

Jax yawned again. 'Nah, just too much…wine.'

'You look awful,' Nita said, offering the statement as though it were a compliment.

'I think you should lie down,' Argento said, now rising from his chair. He took Jax's arm, and the man stood and allowed himself to be led away, not apologising or saying goodbye as he left. I looked over at you, to see what you thought of this whole strange situation, but you seemed preoccupied with pouring some water for us all and wouldn't meet my gaze.

Coffee was brought out by a silent servant while we were waiting, and we sipped it and chatted whilst Douglas resumed his flirting with Nita. When Argento returned, he suggested Nita took you and Douglas for a swim in the pool. Unsure why I hadn't been included in this plan, I was about to say something when Argento turned to me and said, 'Oliver. Would you please join me for an evening stroll?'

I could hardly refuse him and as Nita led you off towards the pool area accompanied by an eager-looking Douglas, I followed Argento down a winding staircase descending from the villa deep into the rocks.

'I'm sorry for that rather tiresome dinner,' Argento said as we made our way down. 'But I hope what I'm about to show you will make up for it.

'What...where are we going?' I asked, feeling confused. Fearful, even.

'It's something important,' he said, 'but I must ask you not to scream.'

Chapter Eight

Chapter Eighteen

THEN

He continued to lead me down the winding stone staircase that disappeared into the shrubbery and trees, looping round the curvature of the outside of the villa. Once the plants were towering around us, I could see a hollow at the bottom and a little door in the side of the villa's wall. Argento unlocked it and stepped inside, holding the door, which appeared to be made of heavy metal, open for me to follow.

Further down we went, now in darkness save for one tiny bulb in the centre of this interior staircase. Are we headed for a cellar? I wondered to myself as I felt the temperature dropping. Or perhaps a dungeon? Maybe this was an elaborate kidnapping, and he was about to tie me up and demand my parents wire him a few million as the price of my freedom. I remember reading a book about the real-life kidnapping of a boy in Italy in the 70s, the son or grandson of a millionaire. They held him in a cave and tried to get a fortune out of his rich relatives, but the family kept holding off paying the ransom. Even though he eventually got away, the kidnappers cut off his ear as a threat of what more they could do with him. As I remembered this, I semi-consciously lifted my hand to one of my own ears, managing to make myself even more afraid than I had been already.

When Argento opened another door and turned on a light, I thought at first I was in some sort of medieval jail, perfectly reconstructed, even down to the iron cells with bars on their doors.

'What is this pl—' I started to say, then I stopped still, the words disappearing as my eyes picked up something. Movement. There appeared to be four separate, sizable cells, each divided by a concrete wall, although all with the same metal doors with bars. The movement had come from the cell at the far end. It wasn't empty.

'Why don't you go and have a look down there,' Argento said, quietly. 'Go on. No harm will befall you, I promise.'

With mounting trepidation, I did as he suggested. My curiosity had been more than piqued. But with each step, there was something that told me I was making a grave error walking across this stretch of gloom towards whatever was in the cell at the end. An error that would cost me dearly.

At last, I reached the metal bars of Cell Number 4. And then took an immediate step back.

A young man lay on the cold stone floor. I almost didn't recognise him at first, the sight being so incongruous, but after a second or two I realised it was Jax. He was naked except for a pair of white designer boxers, along with a gag in his mouth – a ball-gag that appeared to be entirely metal in its construction.

He seemed to be in a state halfway between sleep and consciousness and kept raising his head and moving his hands, then flopping back down again as if drifting back off. With each movement, the chains that were connected to his arms and fixed to the roof jangled and clinked a little.

'Oh my God,' I said, in barely a whisper.

Argento had reached me and stepped forward, surveying the young man with a look of mild interest, as if we were in a zoo. 'As you know, this is Jax Wolf. After suffering his company at dinner – an experience I very much apologise for – you'll know that he is egotistical, arrogant, confident, and generally rather unpleasant. He is thirty years old and was born on the ninth of May 1967 in the London Borough of Havering, and, as he mentioned an hour or two ago, he spends a lot of time in South America and Mexico.'

I stared up at Argento, then back at the figure in the cell. 'Why is he here? Why is he like this?' I asked, taking a step closer. As I did so, the tip of my shoe accidentally hit the metal bars, causing a clang. The prisoner jerked suddenly and tried to scrabble backwards, as if desperate to get away from the sound, but he wasn't able to move far before the chains restricted his movements and he was stuck.

'You might have guessed that Mr Wolf is not a very savoury character, Oliver. Although he has been truthful about the location of his work, he wasn't entirely honest about what his "trade and shipping" company really involves. He implied earlier that I might become an investor in his business. I will not. The true reason for me bringing him to this island has less to do with his business acumen and more to do with the fact that he is, by most measurements, expendable. The world will not miss him. He is, first and foremost, a drug dealer and human trafficker. There are stories I could tell you about his operations, along with his own recreational pursuits, that would paralyse your soul. But I think it's more effective to show you.'

Argento stepped forward and brought out a set of keys. I thought he was about to unlock the barred door, but instead he turned to his right and faced a doorway in the wall at the end of the gallery we were standing in – a door I'd barely registered, so bewitched was I by the spectacle in the cell. The door opened to reveal absolutely nothing – total darkness lay beyond. Even the warm glow of the bare lightbulbs in the cells didn't travel enough to show what the room back there contained, and I didn't ask as Argento stepped forward. I was about to follow, presuming he intended me to venture into the darkness with him, but his frame returned into view within seconds, walking backwards, pulling something with him. It was a metal trolley, with a flat surface upon which sat a large black television and next to it what appeared to be a VCR player and a remote control. On a lower shelf on the trolley was a line of black rectangles, presumably videocassettes. Argento bent down and plugged the set into a wall socket to the right of the doorway and picked up the control.

'During Mr Wolf's operations he regularly does business with many other, well, unsavoury types of people. People who may share similar…*interests*.' He picked up the first of the line of videos and inserted it into the machine.

'What's…what's on the tape?' I asked, my voice trembling a

little. Argento stood motionless for a moment, then turned his head slowly round to face me.

'Terrible things,' he said, in a very quiet voice. He held my gaze for a few seconds more, then pointed the remote at the television.

Chapter Nineteen

THEN

A grey image swam into focus, grainy and indistinct. I took a step nearer, trying to find out what I was seeing. I then took an immediate step back.

'Turn it off,' I said, the words coming out of me in a rush.

Argento did nothing.

'I said, turn it off!' I said, managing to conjure more force in my voice.

Argento calmly raised the control and clicked. The image paused but didn't disappear. It sat there, juddering on the screen.

'I think you now have some idea about what sort of man Jax Wolf is,' Argento said.

I felt the blood within me turning to ice, as if this strange cellar with its relatively neutral temperature was actually a freezer that would eventually chill all sense of life within me. I could hardly move, but I managed to shake my head, just a few centimetres slowly from side to side. I wasn't sure if I was agreeing or disagreeing with him, but it was the only response I was able to give.

'Throughout my life, Oliver, I've succeeded by giving people chances. It hasn't always worked, I grant you, but I think I'm a very good judge of character. I met some people when I was a young man who introduced me to certain aspects of the world that otherwise remain hidden to so-called "ordinary folk". By giving other people the chance to take a similar step, I see this as akin to passing on a gift. Do you understand me, Oliver?'

I shook my head again.

Argento surveyed me, his expression neutral, then reached into his pocket and pulled something out. I stared down at his hand and saw a small case – like a wallet, although slightly thicker and longer, with a zip around the edge. It reminded me of a small shaving kit some men would pack in their travel bags, although this was unmistakably made of snakeskin and looked very expensive. With his other hand, Argento began to unzip the case and opened it out to reveal two objects.

And that's when I understood.

'No,' I said, shaking my head again, more vigorously this time.

'Yes, Oliver. This is a chance – an opportunity – to take a step, a *leap*, into the unknown. You never really know how your body is going to react after an act like this, but you have to trust me that it's going to be *extraordinary*. It won't cause him pain, I promise you. It will be peaceful.'

I stared down at the contents of the case. The small vial of a clear liquid. The syringe with its thin needle. I knew I couldn't do it.

'I need to leave,' I said, suddenly feeling as if I couldn't breathe. I walked away from Argento, down the length of the room, past the other empty cages and over to the door by which we'd come in.

The door was locked.

'I need to get out!' I shouted. But he just stood there, still and silent, maddeningly silent, so I kicked the door furiously and uselessly, resulting in a shooting pain in my foot.

'Oliver, please calm down,' Argento said. 'I promise you, I am not going to hurt you in any way in this room today. Come. Walk back over here and I'll present you with a compromise. All you have to do is listen, and then do nothing. Do you think that's possible?'

My heart pounded, my body tense, my flesh fizzing, like I'd been plunged into acid. But when my eyes met Argento, I found I couldn't escape him. Like a magnet pulled by an invisible force, I ended up turning and walking back to the final cell to stand by him. My body hadn't relaxed; I was still as tense, with sweat breaking out on my forehead; but I felt a slight ease come upon me that I hadn't expected, as if by making the choice to return I had answered a terrifying question within myself – a question that had felt like a brief but acute period of torture before it had been resolved.

'Just stand still. Watch. Do nothing. That's all I ask of you, Oliver,' Argento said calmly.

Then he stepped towards the cell bars and began to unlock the door.

A minute later – though it felt like hours – when we were walking back up the stone steps, through the tall plants and into the dwindling evening light, it hit me what I had become.

An accessory to murder. I wasn't just a witness. I had been part of it. I had nodded to Argento that I was willing to stand there as he inserted the needle first into the silver top of the vial, and then in the gap between two of Jax Wolf's toes on his left foot. I hadn't made any attempt to knock the syringe out of his hand as he did so. Nor had I turned away. I just stared into those widening, pleading, bloodshot eyes. I watched as the life started to leave them. And in doing so became complicit in something I never thought would have touched my life.

Murder.

'Do not worry, Oliver. Mr Wolf's death will be easily put down to the fact that he couldn't resist doing business with some of the most violent and lawless people on the planet. Nothing will be traced back to this island, me or you. Although before we return to the world above, there is one last thing I must show you,' Argento said. 'Return with me to the television, Oliver. Please.'

When I didn't move, he put out a hand. Rested it on my shoulder. I allowed him to gently steer me back towards the TV. I stayed still as he inserted another video cassette into the machine. Waited while the fuzzy image fizzled into focus.

A bedroom. Perhaps a hotel room. Two people on a bed.

'I…I don't want to…' I started to say.

'Watch,' Argento said, and there was something in his voice – a hardness that wasn't there before – that made me instantly fall silent.

The two people on the bed were moving. From what I could make out, one was male and the other female. At first I presumed they were having sex, since they were both naked.

But that wasn't what was happening here. The man was on top of the woman, holding her down, hands around her neck. She was writhing, scratching at his back, the lines she was leaving in his flesh visible even on the grainy footage. Then she grew still. The man stepped off the bed. He was motionless at first, looking at the woman he had just killed. He put his hands to his face. Was he appalled at what he'd just done? Or just out of breath, exhausted from the effort? Then he walked around the bed, over to the phone on the bedside table. Made a call. Then sat on the side of the duvet, facing away from the body. Argento wound the footage forward a little at this point, the whirring noise of the VCR unpleasantly loud, echoing in the silence around us. Then he pressed play, just as the man stood up. He walked out of the frame, although it was clear from a partial reflection in the mirror on the wardrobe that he'd opened the door to the bedroom. Another man walked in, his back to the camera. There was something about this man – his height, his build, his movements – that made me feel like I knew him.

Then it hit me. Hit me with the weight of a thousand worlds crashing into mine, fracturing my present, distorting my past.

The man was my father.

I drew in a breath quickly and looked over at Argento. He was looking at me, then said quietly, 'Look back at the screen, Oliver.'

I continued to watch the silent footage. My father was talking to the younger man. He seemed angry, gesticulating in a way I knew so well. He pointed at scattered clothes on the floor. The younger man started to pull them on hurriedly, while my father went over to the bed. He then began to roll up the woman's body in the duvet.

'What…I don't understand…when…where…'

'Watch' came the instruction again.

So I watched. Watched as my father, now assisted by the other man, lifted the duvet-clad corpse onto the floor, then proceed to wrap it again in the bed sheet. The video footage cut to black, followed by grey fuzz.

'I'm sure you have a lot of questions, so I'm going to give you some answers,' Argento said, 'The young man in the video is named John Foal-Amos. He runs several businesses, most of them fronts for illegal weapons sales. It appears he is known to your father and has relied on him, in the past, for assistance with some difficulties he has encountered.'

I looked back at the TV screen, now blank, then at Argento. 'Difficulties?' I repeated, unsure if it was a question or if I was just coming to turns with how such a simple word could be used to describe something so terrible.

'Now, that's all in the past. Let us talk about the present. Your father has decided not to do business with me. I was going to invest in a project of his, but he's decided to look elsewhere. He is free to do this. But I always find it's best to do some research into the people I'm dealing with. And as you can see, what I found out was quite revealing. Whether you tell your father or not about this, that is up to you,' says Argento. 'But know this: I can show you a dark world that you've never even dreamed of. Come back here next week, and I'll never show this tape to anyone.'

Chapter Twenty

THEN

I didn't speak as I climbed the stone steps back up to the main part of the house. I felt in shock. Dazed. Nauseous, even. Argento remained silent too. I suspect he knew I needed to compute what had just happened. I needed time to order my thoughts. Make sense of everything. Find my way back to you.

When we reached the pool area, I spotted Douglas and Nita in the pool – Douglas underwater and coming to the surface at the far end where Nita was leaning against the side, the shallows coming up to her shoulders. Douglas swam over to the side when he saw us.

'There you are,' he called out. 'We wondered what had become of you.'

I didn't answer him at first – I was puzzled you weren't in the pool with them. For a moment I felt a flicker of panic rise within me. Then I spotted you, right across from the pool, on one of the sun loungers near one of the pillars. I could see your hair was wet, suggesting you had been swimming, but you were fully clothed, and had an odd look on your face that I couldn't quite read. Your eyes came up to meet mine and the look vanished and your familiar grin appeared. I tried to return it, but suddenly an act as simple and commonplace as smiling felt extremely hard – like I was pushing a rock up a hill with the muscles in my cheeks. My resulting expression was probably more of a grimace and I hastily switched my attention to Douglas, who was waving at me, apparently feeling ignored.

'Hello? Oliver? Anyone home?' he called out.

'Yes,' I said, 'Sorry. Argento was…we were…just looking at the garden. You're having fun, I take it?'

My voice sounded false and uneven, but Douglas seemed oblivious. 'It's heaven here,' Douglas said, letting go of the sides and floating on his back, moving his arms through the dappled surface of the water. The warm lighting of the outdoor lamps hanging from hooks between the pillars gave the whole area an otherworldly feel, as if I'd stepped back out into a reality that was altered, foreign. A planet I no longer knew.

'Why don't you come in?' Nita said, calmly, with a slightly seductive tilt to her head.

'No,' I said, more firmly than I meant to. 'I'm…sorry, it's time we left.'

'Oh, really?' Douglas said, allowing his feet to meet the floor of the pool and wading towards me, 'I don't think we need to just yet.'

'Our parents will be worried.'

Douglas frowned, 'Well, that's a bit rich, considering your all-night adventures these days. So I take it you're coming back with me then?' He glanced over at Alastair. I suddenly felt alarmed, as if I'd stumbled down a dead-end. Did I really want to go back to the family villa? Did I want to see my father, after what I had just seen? Was I going to confront him? Tell him everything? Ask him to explain himself? Or never mention any of this to anyone?

I chose the coward's way out. I chose to delay. Delay the time when I would have to see him and make that choice – the choice whether to act as if I didn't know what he'd done or who he'd been involved with in the past, or to tell him I knew what sort of man he really was.

'I'm…going back to Alastair's hostel,' I said, slowly.

In my peripheral vision, I thought I saw Argento's head turn, ever so slowly, to look at me. Perhaps he was interested in how I was dealing with the information I now had. And what I had just experienced.

'So long as that's OK?' I asked you.

'Of course it is,' you replied, your expression blank but your eyes keenly trained upon me like spotlights, searching inside, trying to glean what was going on.

'So…I think we should go. Now.' I sounded a little blunt, probably rude, to Douglas's ears, and he certainly seemed confused at my behaviour.

I looked over at you again, hoping you would have a view, that you could tell I needed to get away from this villa and off this island right now.

'Let's go,' you said. You knew at once what I needed and I felt a rush of gratitude to you right then.

To my surprise, Argento also came to my rescue. 'I think this would be a good idea,' he said. 'I'll make sure the boat is waiting for you.' As he turned to go, he looked at me for a fraction of a second. And in that fraction, he smiled. Then he was gone.

We barely spoke during the boat ride back. Douglas seemed relaxed and happy, leaning back with his arms behind his head as we sped away from the island, as if all was right with the world. I wish I could have done the same. You were also quiet, although you gave my leg a squeeze as you got up to climb off when we began to dock. You could tell there was something going on.

When we reached the shore and disembarked, Douglas seemed keen to keep the evening going. 'We should go for drinks!' he declared enthusiastically. I didn't say anything, just looked at you, then back at my brother. Douglas got the hint.

'Ah, sorry. I guess you guys want…err…some time alone, don't you?' He patted me on the shoulder. 'Have a good night, youngling.' He winked. 'See you both tomorrow.'

I felt slightly bad, then, as he began his walk back along the seafront in the direction of the family villa, the direction of Dad's moodiness, Mum's neuroticism and the stark bedroom where he would spend his night alone. Part of me wanted to call out to him, to tell him I'd changed my mind, that I wanted to come home with him. But didn't. I'd made my choice. I knew this evening was going to be hard. And I'd chosen to spend it with you.

Silence fell as we climbed the stairs at the hostel and went into your dorm. Once we'd closed the door, you turned to me. 'Are…are you OK?'

I felt a chill start to spread down from my neck across my

back, even though the night was a warm one. 'Yes, fine,' I said quickly. Too quickly. You raised your eyebrows. I decided to change the subject. 'I was actually going to ask you the same thing. You looked a bit…I don't know…left out at the villa. I thought you'd have been in the pool with Douglas and Nita.'

You nodded, slowly. You looked as if you were trying to decide whether to say something. Then eventually you opened your mouth and said. 'I was at first…but it was….I don't know, a bit awkward.' You paused, frowning, then continued. 'Nita was all over Douglas. It was clear she fancied him and I just felt like a third wheel. Which I feel bad for, because Douglas probably feels like that with us, sometimes. But all the same, she was…sort of blatant.'

'Blatant?' I said, 'Well, I'm not surprised. She flirted with him when she came to deliver fruit to our villa. And she made it clear she wanted him to come with us to the island today.'

You smiled a little. 'Well, I think she well and truly got what she hoped for.'

I realised what you meant. 'Oh…I see…you mean they…'

'Yeah, I think they…well…did it. Or maybe they fooled around – I'm not sure, but something occurred between them.'

'Weren't you there?' I asked, not sure how much of my brother's activities with Nita I wanted to hear about.

'I went to dry off. When I got back to the terrace, Douglas was sitting by the edge of the pool with his back to me and he had his underpants down – he pulled them up quickly, presumably when he heard me coming back out to the pool. Nita had been in a black bathing suit before, but she was suddenly wearing absolutely nothing.'

'Did they say anything?' I asked, finding something

disquieting in the story, but I wasn't sure what.

'No,' you said, 'Douglas just slid back into the pool and started doing lengths, as if nothing had occurred. Nita looked at me and smiled and asked if I was coming back in, but I said I was going to watch the sunset.'

You lay back on your bed and said, 'I guess Nita's a beautiful woman. Why shouldn't your brother have a bit of fun?'

I lay on one of the spare beds next to yours, staring at the ceiling. 'I guess,' I said. I began to realise why I didn't like the idea of Douglas and Nita. After what had happened between me and Argento – what I had witnessed in the dungeon – I didn't want Douglas having a connection to that island or anyone who resided on it. Even though he was my big brother, I felt a sudden surge of worry about him – a protective instinct, wanting to keep him safe from the strange horrors he knew nothing about.

Eventually I heard you wander off to brush your teeth, but I stayed still. Tense. Unsure. Like the wiring of my brain was firing, fusing, then reconnecting.

I sat up when you came back in. You pulled off your clothes and asked if I wanted to do something.

'Not tonight,' I said. 'I think I need to sleep.'

When you asked again what was wrong, I assured you there was nothing. Too much sun, too much wine, I told you.

'This doesn't have anything to do with you going off with Argento after dinner?' you asked.

'No,' I lied. 'Nothing. I just need to sleep.'

So I slept. And as I slept, I dreamed. But they weren't pleasant dreams.

Chapter Twenty-One

THEN

Over the week that followed, I was disconcerted by how quickly we fell back into a routine similar to the one we had before, although now with my brother as a more regular presence. The most remarkable thing was that Douglas suddenly didn't seem to be in any hurry to go back to England.

'So, do I take it you're staying for now?' I asked cautiously two days after our last visit to the island.

'Well, there's no rush, is there?' he shrugged, not meeting my eyes.

'You seemed pretty set on the idea before.'

He didn't reply.

'Douglas?' I pushed, confused about why he was now evading my questions. He just put on his shades so I couldn't continue to make eye contact.

'Relax, Oliver. Just enjoy the sun.'

'*Enjoy the sun*?' I couldn't help laughing. But as I lay back on the beach to do exactly that, your arm around me, I watched Douglas sitting on his towel, slightly apart from us, staring out to sea in the direction of Cruciamen Island. Almost out of sight, but not, apparently, out of his thoughts. Nor out of mine.

Both of you seemed to be content to spend most days relaxing on the beach, or sometimes the three of us would take long walks and have relaxed lunches overlooking the sea. Things, in any other circumstances, would have been wonderfully calm and relaxed. But for me, everything had changed.

Douglas noticed it first – or at least he was the one to draw attention to it. He asked me why I kept slipping into a dreamlike state, and at one point at dinner on the Tuesday evening he waved his hands in front of my face and said, 'Are we boring you, youngling?' I snapped back to the present and winced, hearing the nickname and finding it embarrassing to have it uttered in front of you. At least the embarrassment momentarily shifted my attention away from what had been preoccupying it. The cells, the chains, the look in Jax Wolf's eyes as life was extinguished. It was as though I'd seen a particularly disturbing film that had started to bleed into reality. Or a dream I'd woken up from but couldn't escape every time I let my mind wander.

'Perhaps we should go back to see Mum for a bit,' I suggested. I didn't want you to think I was tired of our time together, but I'd begun to feel our current lifestyle wasn't helping my thoughts.

'Go back if you need to,' you said, laying an understanding hand on my arm.

Douglas, however, was less enthusiastic. 'Do we have to?

You do know the only reason they've stopped scrutinising what you're up to is because they think you're off having racy summer flings and are too squeamish to think about it. I don't have that shield to hide behind.'

'I'm not sure I'd put it like that,' I said.

'Well, as soon as we're in, Dad will berate us for something or other.'

This sent me spiralling off again. How would I spend the coming weeks, months, years looking at my father knowing what he'd been a part of? I ended up getting caught in loops, my own moral maze, about what he had done. It was like a trial, with defence and prosecution. The defence said he hadn't killed anyone, and perhaps he was clearing up the crime scene because he had no choice; maybe the people he was working with were a threat to him, to us, his family. The prosecution reminded me that he had been an accessory to the murder of a young woman, no matter how one spun it. A young woman who was someone's daughter or sister or wife or girlfriend or mother.

'I wonder what Nita's up to now,' Douglas said, sighing.

'Whatever she's paid to do,' I muttered.

Douglas leaned back in his chair, surveying me with a slight frown, 'Do you have something against her?'

I sighed and said, 'Look, Doug, I know you're...attracted to her. But don't you think you should let things be? If she's being paid by Argento, perhaps you should leave her alone. Let her get on with whatever is going on between them.'

I felt you shift a little next to me. Perhaps you didn't want to be present when this difficult subject came up.

'Aren't you being a bit…I don't know…judgemental?' Douglas said, sounding a little hurt.

'Aren't you being a little naïve?' I retorted, my words sounding harsher than I intended. 'Did you fuck her, last Saturday? You did, didn't you? And when you were fucking her, did you at any point think she wasn't doing that because she *wanted* to, she was doing that because she may have been *ordered* to? Doesn't that bother you?'

'I'm going to get the bill,' you said, standing up. Neither Douglas nor I said anything, just glared at each other.

Once you'd walked away, Douglas lowered his voice and said, 'For the record, we didn't fuck, she just…well…you know—'

'No, actually I don't and I don't want to. I just don't think you should be getting any more involved than you are.'

'What's prompted this?' Douglas said, raising his hands in the air in exasperation. 'I've done my best to be friendly to your…your…man friend, boyfriend, lover, whatever you want to call him. I've defended your lifestyle choices to Mum and Dad—'

'*Lifestyle choices*?' I repeated, getting properly angry now.

'Sorry, no, bad phrasing. I didn't mean that.'

'Oh, I think you did.'

Douglas grabbed my arm. 'No, I didn't, and you know that. Please don't make this into something it's not. You know I support you and love you, all I'm asking is that you pay me the same compliment and stop your sudden disapproval. I…I really like her…and I know it's not going to last for ever, I know the situation she's in isn't ideal…but I just want to see where it leads, if only for the summer. OK?'

His expression was so earnest and determined, I found I couldn't fight any more. I nodded, slowly. 'OK.'

He smiled and released my arm, giving it a pat. 'Friends again?'

'Always friends,' I said, returning his smile, trying to make mine as natural as possible.

As the days went by, we didn't speak specifically about the island, but it seemed we'd already decided we would be going back again. To Douglas, at least, it seemed like a non-negotiable certainty. It felt like we were just passing the days, waiting for Saturday to arrive. I tried to read, but it was as if all the joy had gone out of it all.

On the Wednesday, after my thoughts had tortured me for four days, I strongly considered going to the police. But something told me not to get mixed up with it all. I hadn't done anything wrong. I hadn't killed anyone. I hadn't committed a crime. But I hadn't done anything to stop one occurring. I hadn't reported it when it had occurred. That, itself, put me in a difficult situation. And what if Argento made good on his threat? I imagined the horror and shame my parents would feel, going through a police investigation, the stories in the press, God forbid a trial in court if it got that far. No matter how much they annoyed me, no matter how many times their arguments and criticisms and eccentricities annoyed me, they were still my family. And I loved them.

Eventually I decided on two things: not to say anything and not to go again. I would stay away from whatever was going on in Argento's villa. Stay clear of whatever mind games he was trying to play with us. Put what happened last weekend behind me. And soon, with the passing of time, it would become a bad dream. It was a risk, disobeying his instructions, but perhaps less risky than going to the police. A compromise, of sorts – a compromise I would try to live with, whatever the outcome.

The days started to pass frighteningly quickly, bringing us up to three weeks since our arrival in Greece. It was as if someone had sped up the cycles of the sun and the moon, and when I woke on Saturday morning I said to you, 'Is it Friday?'

'No, Saturday,' you said, giving me a kiss on the cheek, then moving over to get on top of me. 'And I think it's time for your weekend wake-up call.' You started to kiss down my stomach, disappearing under the duvet, but I put out my hands to stop him. 'No, stop, I…I don't think…I think I'm ill.'

You pulled yourself back up out of the covers to look at me, your golden hair practically glowing in the morning sun. 'Ill?' you asked, and put a hand out to my forehead. 'You don't feel like you have a temperature.'

'I think I might,' I said, 'I think…I feel like I've got flu or something like that.'

You stared at me and I started to find your gaze impossible to hold. I was lying to you. And I could tell that you knew. You just didn't know why. Could never know why. There was no possibility of me telling you why I could never go back to that island. No way I was going to let what happened there infect what we had.

If only I had seen that through my actions – and through my lies – things were already becoming infected. I could have told you everything, there and then, and explained why we should never go back, why we should leave Greece, or rent a cabin somewhere, head to the forests of Eastern Europe or emigrate to Australia, anything to get away from the sinister reach of Argento.

But I didn't. I allowed you to head off to the beach with Douglas, even after you'd offered to stay in the room and take care of me. When the two of you returned to convince me to go to the island with them, I declined.

'Maybe you should stay back, too,' I said to Douglas, a weak, last-ditch attempt to keep him with me.

'That would be...I don't know...rude,' he said. 'We're expected.'

I wanted to remind him that the original invitation to visit hadn't initially included him. But I could see the hunger in his eyes. I knew why he wanted to get back there. He was under Nita's spell, and from what you had described, he was keen for a repeat – or a continuation – of last time.

I couldn't help but feel a bit hurt when you disappeared without entering into the discussion. You didn't try asking me to come, instead you seemed perfectly happy to spend the evening with Douglas, as if my lack of attendance didn't really change anything.

I briefly left your dorm room to have a bite to eat at a café by myself, then returned with a bottle of wine and drank it by myself as the evening light turned to night. I must have drifted off at some point, as I woke to hear footsteps and the door opening. You came in. I turned over to look at you. I could tell at once something was wrong. You, who never avoided anyone's eyes, seemed determined not to look at me.

'Did you have a good time?' I asked quietly in the darkness.

You didn't reply for a moment as you tugged off the last of your clothes and then got into bed. Then you said, 'Yes. I just need to sleep.'

I don't know if either of us slept much that night. And by the time the morning light started to come through the thin curtains, I had worked it out. I pulled the covers off me and sat on the edge of the bed, watching, waiting. As soon as you opened your eyes, I started to speak.

'He took you to the dungeon, didn't he?'

You turned to face me. You looked pale. Tense. Instantly alert.

'Yes.'

I paused, then asked my second question. 'And who did you watch him murder?'

You let a few seconds pass, then said one word. 'Nita.'

Chapter Twenty-Two

NOW

We've been sat outside the wellness centre for so long that the autumn chill brings a halt to our conversation. I became aware of the temperature dropping when the clouds of our breath became more distinct, and now I can practically hear the sounds of the moisture on the leaves turning to frost. We decide to move inside the hotel. I'm not sure what we have in mind as we move through the doors inside to the warmly lit interior. The canteen, maybe? It seems odd – no, incomprehensible – that we would be able to sit sipping coffees or high-vitamin smoothies together whilst catching up on the old days. Not that I'm particularly keen to speak about the old days. I'm aware how difficult, or potentially dangerous, my own situation is. I just don't know how aware you are.

'I know where we can warm up,' you say. 'Follow me.'

You lead me along the left-hand side of the main corridor then down some stairs to the underground floors. The signs on the walls make it clear we're heading to the gym, sauna, spa and pool. The pool has a large red warning sign up warning users that there was no lifeguard on duty. Now I'm heading towards the poolside with you, I regret not coming down here more when it was just me. When I didn't have this disruption in whatever sort of peace I was trying to find here.

'We can't swim,' I say to you as you survey the empty pool, the surface completely flat. 'Or at least, I can't. I haven't got my swim things. They're back in my room.' I glance at your hands – you're definitely not holding a bag or anything containing trunks.

A small smile appears on your face. 'I don't think that's bothered you before…'

I don't return your smile. 'Skinny dipping in a secluded cove is a bit different to an indoor swimming pool.'

You don't say anything. You simply turn away from the pool's edge and walk off in the direction of the men's changing room. I get the feeling you want me to follow you, so I choose not to. I sit down awkwardly, still in my coat, on the edge of one of the loungers at the side. It has a little spotlight above it – a warm tone, in contrast to the dark blue lighting around the main pool area – and I'm tempted to just lie back and go to sleep. But I don't. I sit there. Waiting. And barely a minute later the door to the men's changing area opens and you return, now without your clothes, with just a towel around your waist. I look up at you as you walk over, coming round to the lounger next to mine.

'Are you naked under there?' I ask, nodding at the towel.

'Why?' you ask, 'are you…interested?'

I don't answer. After a moment, you smile. 'Relax. I've got my pants on.'

You settle on the lounger, lifting your long, tanned legs onto the padded material and stretching them out. I feel a stirring of desire within me. I try to tell it to go to hell, but it doesn't work. I sit for a while, steadily feeling warmer and warmer in my coat. After a few minutes I can't bear it anymore and get up. You don't ask where I'm going.

I return after a few moments, minus my clothes, stripped down to my underwear like you, with one of the thick, pleasingly soft towels wrapped around me.

'Come and sit, Oliver,' you call over to me. I feel a little irritated by your tone, as if I'm a child or an employee, someone you can order about. Perhaps returning back from the dead makes one feel a bit superior.

'I'm still interested in why you're here, Oliver,' you ask, as if our conversation has been a lot more fluid and friendly than it actually has been.

'I told you,' I reply, testily.

'No, actually, you haven't.'

I take a deep breath. 'I…if I tell you this, you've got to tell me everything.'

'Everything?' you ask, a smile playing around your mouth once again. You're enjoying yourself. And it makes me angry.

'Yes. Everything.'

Chapter Twenty-Three

THEN

'Tell me about Nita.'

I said the words forcefully and saw something shift in your face. It was almost like relief. As if part of you had been trying to make peace with keeping what you had experienced to yourself. And now you didn't have to do that. A release had been offered, and I could see how willing you were to grab hold of it. You don't have to enter this dark future alone. Prompted by this thought, I held out my hand. You looked down for a few seconds, then took it. 'Tell me,' I said again.

So you told me. Not there in your dorm. We made our way outside, and I was surprised how grey the morning light was, how dark the dawn had remained, how the sun had been extinguished. It was the first grey day we'd had – or at least, the first that stayed in my memory. Dark clouds on the horizon suggested rain was coming and although the air wasn't exactly cold, the normal all-encompassing heat had vanished. You and I walked past the shops, down towards the steps that led to the beach, and followed the coast along until we eventually came to the alcove in the rocks we had come to think of as our own. I was glad that we'd gone there – a place where it was just us away from the rest of the world. Once you finished your story, though, I began to regret our choice of location. I felt that it had been tainted by what you told me.

You told me how you'd arrived on the island with Douglas, and Argento was waiting. You described how Nita was standing with him, fully clothed this time. Argento gave her to Douglas – that was how you worded it. 'Gave her', as if she was an item that could be transferred rather than a person. The two of them went inside the villa while you ate and drank with Argento. You assumed they'd gone to find a bedroom and said you could hear the low moans of Douglas and Nita having sex throughout your meal with Argento, and how he didn't seem fazed by this. Didn't even comment on it.

'I knew Douglas was only staying because he was keen to see Nita again,' I said.

You nodded. 'He spoke about her a lot. Described her as "intoxicating". And I suppose he had a point. She is rather…*was* rather…striking.'

'Was she?' I asked, looking at you. 'Was she *striking* when you watched her die?'

I didn't know why I was adopting such a bitter tone, as if I blamed you for what happened. Perhaps I was repulsed by your experience more than my own because it involved someone we knew – or at any rate someone we'd spent some time with. At least for me it had been a stranger. Jax Wolf had been a man I'd barely spoken two words to, someone with no connection to me, from a life that bore no resemblance to mine.

'How could you have watched while he killed Nita?' I asked you. The wind had whipped up and you swiped up at your forehead to remove your fringe from your eyes. You looked over at the cave behind us and nodded at it. 'Come on, let's shelter in there.'

We walked inside and huddled against one of the walls, watching the sky darken from the arched entrance. A curtain of rain started to fall seconds later, mixing with the wind and creating a roaring sound. We moved back a little until we came to a large, dry, flattish rock and sat down.

'Carry on,' I said.

So you continued your horror story. Told me how, later in the evening, Douglas had returned to the table, flushed and happy. How he'd stayed and drunk wine and mentioned Nita was having a lie-down. He went for a post-coital swim whilst you were led away by Argento. Down the steps.

'He had her in a cage on a bed,' you said, not looking right at me, but instead staring at the sandy floor of the cave where a trickle of water was starting to run in.

'Did he inject her with a clear liquid from a vial?' I asked.

You frowned, then eventually nodded.

I guessed what you were thinking. You hadn't yet asked me, but I'd known from the moment I asked the initial question, back in the hostel, that you would work it out. And now it was time for you to ask your ultimate question.

'Who died when you were there?'

I said nothing.

'It was Jax Wolf, wasn't it? When he grew tired after dinner?'

I took a deep breath, then replied. 'Not yet. I will tell you, but first there are more things I need to understand. I need some…justification.'

Still frowning, you opened your mouth, then closed it again. Then you said 'You mean…why…the reason…'

'The reason Argento gave for Nita's death. He must have given a reason.'

I felt my hands starting to shake. The words had finally made it clear to me the full horror of the situation we'd wandered into.

'When Argento showed me down to that…that place,' you said, 'where she was asleep on the bed…behind the bars…he explained she had a dark past. A *very* dark past. Long before she was employed by him for the summer. Long before she became an escort. He then told me that she had done…terrible things.'

'What sort of terrible things?' I asked, not sure that I actually wanted to know.

'That she allowed two of her siblings and parents to burn in a house fire in order to get the insurance money. He said she then…rented out…her surviving younger brother to older men for sex and kept the cash. Argento proved this…he played me tapes…'

You started crying at this point. Not racking sobs or howls of pain. Just silent tears, falling down your smooth, beautiful face, and they continued as if no comfort in the world could stop them. 'And then he offered me the chance to inject her.… I refused, but I did watch.' You nodded a little, almost like a child admitting their part in a deed that shames them. 'Yes…I did watch.'

You explain that you and Douglas came back in the boat,

with Douglas knowing nothing about what happened – that the woman he had made love to an hour earlier was no longer living.

'There's something else. About…about Douglas,' you said. 'I think Argento knew I would go back and tell you about all this. He told me to tell you that the condoms Douglas used had been kept. And that it would be very easy for one of two things to happen.' He sniffed and drew in a deep breath, then continued. 'Either we say nothing and return to the island, or Douglas's DNA finds its way to a crime scene in the UK at some point in the near future.'

I should have known this was on the cards. That the threat of blackmail towards my father wouldn't be enough for him. That Argento needed something more tangible, more immediate, in order to manipulate me.

'That doesn't stop you,' I said, swallowing, trying to control my emotions. 'He hasn't got a hold over you. You don't owe any loyalty to my brother.'

I wasn't sure if I was testing him then, or just stating facts. Getting them out in the open. But he looked at me solemnly and said, 'I would never do that to you.'

I knew it would be my turn next. My turn to relive what had happened when Argento had taken me to that dungeon. So I told him everything that had occurred with Jax Wolf. How he hadn't been on a bed, but rather chained up, shifting, twitching. And how I'd watched him die, the same way you had watched the life leave Nita.

I started crying too as I recounted my story, and once I had finished we wrapped our arms around each other and huddled as the storm raged outside the cave. 'They deserved it, didn't they?' I whispered in your ear, needing to hear you say it, to tell me I was right. Without hesitation, you said back: 'Yes. They deserved it.'

We sat there, our embrace lasting what felt like many lifetimes, the two of us bonded together in the dark truth of our experiences. Perhaps it would have been best if the cave had flooded, if the water had swelled or the rainfall had continued its steady march towards us and swept us and our confusing new lives out to sea, never to be seen again. But when we broke apart, the ground was still dry. The rain had stopped. The storm had passed. And from the entrance of the cave, a beam of sunlight was shining, bathing everything in a gold light. Although it was the afternoon, it felt like a new dawn.

Chapter Twenty-Four

THEN

A fter that point, we didn't really look back. Not then, anyway. It was like we'd reached an understanding that the past was in the past. Our next moral challenge would come when we had to decide whether to return to the island. But before that question arrived, we – or rather I – had another problem to deal with: my brother.

I had wondered if he should be told, in some ambiguous way, that he wouldn't be seeing Nita again. It turned out, however, that Argento had prepared for that. Shortly before their dinner, Douglas said Nita and he had gone off together 'for some time alone' and afterwards she had said that she had been suddenly called back to America, and would be leaving the following day.

The effect this had on Douglas's mood was instant and troubling. He became moody, irritable, and started to avoid our company. On one of the few occasions I went back to the family villa, he kept to his room, muttering that he was thinking of resuscitating last week's plan of going back to

England now that the lure of Nita had been extinguished – or at least was now out of his reach. After I had heard about the barely veiled threat made towards him by Argento, I was keen for him never to visit the island again. And if ending our holiday was the best way to secure this, I had no choice but to go along with it. So I told him I understood. I even suggested I would follow at some point before the end of the summer, making myself sound more certain than I was.

When I came out of his room, one afternoon, I met my father on the stairs. He asked, 'He still in one of his strops?'

I nodded, but before I could say anything, the bedroom door behind me flew open and Douglas appeared, looking furious. 'Why don't you come out and say it, Dad? You fucking hate us and think we're a waste of space.'

My father looked shocked. 'I've never said that!'

'Well, you act like it.'

'Well, is it any surprise when you behave like a spoilt teenager half the time?' Dad said, getting properly angry himself now.

'Christ, I'm sick of this place.'

'Doug,' I said, 'I'm sorry that Nita had to…leave Greece.' I found saying her name difficult, but I tried to push down the shaky feeling I had and pressed on. 'But you knew it wasn't going to last for ever.'

'What do you mean?' Dad barked, then he looked at me, 'Is this to do with that…that…prostitute you alluded to, Oliver? Have you been in contact…have you been seeing…?' He stared from one of us to the other. Douglas also turned to me. 'What have you said?'

'Nothing!' I protested. 'Dad, just…just leave this, I can handle it.'

'Handle it? You mean handle *me*?' Douglas said. 'I thought you were on my side.' He went back into his room and I heard things being moved around. I opened the door to see he had his suitcase open on the bed and he'd started to throw clothes into it.

'Doug, look, I didn't mean that,' I started to say, just as I heard my mother calling, 'Hello? What's happening? Why is there shouting?'

'Nothing,' my dad called down. He walked into the bedroom and looked at Douglas hurriedly packing. 'Now both of you listen to me,' he said, holding up a hand. I was alarmed to see it was trembling. 'I don't want either of you to be in contact with…that man. Do you understand me? I don't care if you've taken a fancy to that cheap hooker of his—'

'Don't use words like that,' Douglas snapped, pushing the lid down on his case. 'And you needn't worry. There's no chance of me seeing her anymore.' He picked up his case and carried it out of the room. 'I'm going to call a taxi and go home.'

'Doug, wait,' I said.

'You're not leaving!' Mum called up from the bottom of the stairs.

'I am,' he said as he started his descent. 'I'm sorry, Mum, but I've had enough. Of everything. It's time for me to go home.'

. . .

I went with him to the airport. I felt I owed him that. I wasn't sure how cross he was with me and how much was the fallout from his row with Dad. It felt like something had shifted between us and he said very little during the drive. As we were approaching the airport, though, I noticed him watching me closely. Before he got out, he turned to me properly and said, 'Oliver…'

I waited, then said 'Yes?' wondering what he was about to say. He looked pained, as if he didn't know how to tell me something.

'How serious are you with Alastair? It is…it's just a casual thing, right?'

Whatever I thought he was going to say, I hadn't expected this. 'Why?'

'Just…I don't know. Nothing here lasts for ever, you do realise that? This is all just a holiday. I… don't want you getting hurt too.'

I nodded, and assured him that whatever happened, I'd be fine. I hoped by saying it I would make it true.

He left then, giving me a hug goodbye and disappearing into the airport. I took the taxi back, but not to the villa. I took it to you, to the hostel, where I found you waiting for me.

'So, what now?' you asked when we were back together, facing each other.

I knew what you were asking. I knew what lay behind that question.

An image of the island floated into my mind. Bobbing up and down, as though I was being carried along on rough waters, getting rougher as the island came closer.

'Let's go to our favourite cove.'

162

You probably knew I was dodging the real subtext of what you were asking, but you still nodded and smiled at me. But I knew, deep down, what you wanted. You wanted to return to the island. Return to Argento. Return to whatever dark spectacles he had in store for us next.

Would I have agreed to go, if there had been no connection between Argento and my family, if no danger of blackmail existed, if I had been completely free to walk away? I didn't know. And the fact I didn't know troubled me.

Chapter Twenty-Five

THEN

We didn't talk about it explicitly for the rest of the week. The question remained dodged. The decision we both had to make went unmade. We fell into our old habits, perhaps in the hope that it would instil a sense of normality into our lives. Although I wondered, even then, if that was really what we wanted. If we had wanted normality, we'd have tried to get out of the situation we'd found ourselves in. I would have faced the consequences, told my father everything, potentially changed the course of my family's future. I wish I could say that my decisions then were done entirely to protect my parents – especially my mother – from that fallout. But it wouldn't be true. True in part. But not entirely. I had become intoxicated by the danger, by the strange, dark world I had stepped into. And the fact that you wanted to return made me all the more keen to.

Then we reached Friday evening. We had to decide what to do. That night, we lay in bed and again fantasised about leaving, about going to Germany or even further, Canada perhaps or the United States. Spending the approaching autumn in Long Island or New England, watching the trees turn golden.

'All that can happen one day,' you said. 'But I think we both know it's not going to just yet.'

'Why?' I asked, knowing the answer.

You didn't reply. You didn't need to.

So we caught the boat the next day, in the early evening. I was trembling as I stepped aboard and you took my hand. By the time we arrived at the little jetty and I saw Argento waiting for us, I had stopped shaking. I was calmer. Prepared. I was ready for what awaited us.

'Alastair, it's good to see you. I hope you are well,' Argento said as you got off the boat ahead of me. Our host took your hands in his and kept them clasped and looked into your eyes. The intensity was plain to see, as if he was scanning your soul, searching for something in your eyes. Whatever he was looking for or whatever test was being carried out, it seemed you passed, as Argento's smile spread wide and he released your hands and said, 'Good, good.'

He then turned to me. 'Oliver,' he said, 'I was very sorry not to see you last weekend.'

He left a gap for me to speak, perhaps wondering if I had an excuse. I felt like a slightly strict teacher had just asked me why my homework was late. He stayed silent for such a long time, with you standing there beside him, not looking at me, that eventually I felt so awkward I had to say something.

'I'm…glad to be back.'

He looked at me, hard in the eyes as he'd done with you. I felt a flicker of irritation at first. But as Argento stared at me, I felt my sense of calm returning. He wasn't angry with me – or at least he showed no visible signs of it. He was just trying to gauge my position, and within seconds his smile widened as it had done with you and he had taken my hands in his, almost without me realising. My temperature changed; I felt cold all of a sudden. I realised I was making a firm choice here. A definite decision to continue down this dark path.

'I hope you both have good appetites today,' Argento said. 'We have an Italian chef visiting and he is going to prepare the finest carbonara you'll ever taste. And I have two guests joining us that I'm looking forward to introducing you to. We shall talk and dine and eat marvellous food. I hope this sounds acceptable to you both.'

I nodded. 'I am rather hungry.'

I wasn't saying yes to the pasta. I was saying yes to something else. And Argento knew that.

We were again led through the villa out to the more open area by the pool, although something had changed. For a second I wondered what, trying to work out what was different about the place. Then I realised. The sun loungers were empty. The water undisturbed. Nita was no longer there.

As promised, though, there were two new guests for us to meet, and they stood at the edge of the balcony, overlooking the full and fecund gardens below. I looked up and saw a man and a woman. They appeared to be a little older than we were – young-ish, but perhaps in their early to mid-thirties. The woman was talking quite loudly to the man in a tight, posh voice, saying something along the lines of 'It's all very lovely and everything, but I couldn't be dealing with the faff of all the upkeep.'

The man nodded, then noticed they were no longer alone. He turned to look at us and smiled. 'Hello there,' he said. His companion stopped talking and turned too.

'I'm sorry to interrupt,' said Argento, 'but I wanted to introduce Oliver and Alastair. They are staying in Santorini and I asked them to dine with us. They are…friends of my family.'

The two guests were introduced as Mr and Mrs Greene. Both were exceptionally good-looking and well dressed – he in a cream blazer, pale-blue shirt and chinos, and she in a navy-blue summer dress. The man was friendly and welcoming, shaking our hands and remarking what a magnificent location this was for a dinner on a summer's evening. The woman was friendly to a point, but clearly seemed puzzled by our presence. To her we must have seemed like two random – and rather casually dressed – young men, and I wondered if she had presumed they would be dining with Argento alone.

We made slightly awkward small talk to start with, then were taken round to the table at the side of the veranda for our meal. Mrs Greene ('oh, call me Katherine, please') spoke a lot about what life was currently like in London and how they had been discussing where to buy a holiday home. 'I remain unconvinced,' she said. 'I mean, London can be absolute torture half the time, but I'm not sure Greece would be any different. All the tourists, of course. And the locals aren't much better.'

'I've always found the locals of Santorini to be nothing less than charming,' Argento said, pleasantly.

'I'm sure they are,' Mr Greene – Harry – said, smiling.

'Well, as I said, I remain unconvinced. Although I do think we need to find somewhere away from where we are now. It's truly dire.'

'Whereabouts in London do you live?' Alastair asked.

'Chelsea,' said Katherine.

'And Chelsea is truly dire?' I asked, wondering if our definitions of 'dire' differed.

'Oh, it is, honestly. It used to be perfect. Well, nowhere is perfect of course, and there's been that ghastly brutalist estate in World's End for ages now, but it's just…well…it's about the *class* of people. I mean, we've had a family of *lottery winners* from Stoke move into a house on our square. Imagine!'

Alastair and I nodded as if we sympathised or had any experience of the changing residents of Chelsea.

'What is it you do for work?' Alastair asked.

'Oh, we're in financial management. Hedge funds, ISAs, it's all very boring.'

'Don't talk yourself down, darling. It makes you sound like a socialist,' Katherine said, then laughed, as if what she said was hilarious.

I knew why they were there. I could tell you did too. It felt strange, knowing something like that whilst watching them both talking and eating and showing off. Much like Jax Wolf, I thought. I was surprised to find I didn't feel pity, not in the way I would have expected. I think, by being out of control, knowing the mechanism was already in motion, gave me sufficient distance, allowing me to sit back and watch this couple living out their last hours on this earth in blissful ignorance. It was a strange experience. But not a terrible one.

The carbonara was indeed delicious. You seemed to think so too, clearing your plate even quicker than me. Or perhaps you were just in a hurry for the games to begin.

It was towards the end of dessert when the yawning started. Katherine tried to apologise, saying it must be the heat. Harry said he also felt tired, blaming jet lag, even though they had presumably only flown from the UK. After these first signs, Argento suggested you and I take a walk around the gardens, which we did without question or pause. As we meandered through the tree-lined walkways, I asked you when you thought we should go back. 'Let's give it another ten or fifteen minutes,' you said.

When the time came, we didn't prevaricate. I didn't try to extend the walk, to put off the moment we knew would come, when we'd walk down that winding stone staircase, leading down round the outside of the villa, deep into the undergrowth. We went meekly, silently, without fuss. The only thing that made us stop, briefly and only once, was when you laid your hand on my back as we stepped through the door into the dungeon. I don't know if it was a gesture of comfort, or encouragement, or comradeship. Or all three. Whatever it was, it made me feel safe. I wasn't alone.

Once again, all the cells were empty apart from the last.

I looked inside.

Then I looked at you.

You were completely still. Completely silent. If anything about the sight before you caused you distress or alarm, there wasn't a single thing in your appearance that could have alerted me to it.

But then again, the same may have been true of me. I

wasn't trembling. I wasn't feeling nauseous. To any observer I could be walking into a library or a shop or an art gallery.

I stared down at the two people in the cage. They were slumped against a wall, close together. Their mouths were filled with ball gags, just as Jax Wolf's had been, and they too had been stripped, Harry to a pair of blue briefs and Katherine to a black bra and slip. They appeared to be sound asleep, unaware they were about to be plunged into a nightmare. Without warning, Argento kicked the bars of the cell, resulting in a dull clanging sound reverberating around the basement walls. The two flinched and whimpered, eyes opening for a moment. Katherine's head lolled forwards. Harry opened his eyes again straightaway and started making a sound, as if he was trying to say something. As he moved, the chains they were attached to made an unpleasant scraping sound that reminded me of both an electrical saw and fingers on a blackboard. Argento saw me wince and said, 'As before, Oliver, I ask you not to waste any pity on these two individuals.' He turned round to look at them. 'It's probably best if I tell you more about them because, like the previous guest you met, they have been rather economical with the truth. First, the facts that you know. They are indeed a married couple. They are indeed residents of West London. Mr Greene is thirty-three years of age and was born in Chiswick. Mrs Greene is also thirty-three and was born and grew up in a large townhouse on Chester Square in Belgravia. They met at Cambridge University and decided to go into business with each other. Business became romance. If I can say one thing in their favour, it's this: they are really clever about money.'

'I would hope so, if they're involved in wealth management

and financial advice,' you said, and I was struck by how normally you made the comment, as if you and Argento were surveying a painting together or remarking on an interesting view.

'Exactly so. Mr Greene became quite an expert at shell companies. Companies within companies, all based offshore, with an element remaining on the British mainland that looks perfectly ordinary, unremarkable. Mrs Greene has a natural skill at networking. Together, they built up a considerable network of companies, all of them apparently respectable.'

'What did these companies do?' you asked, taking a step towards the bars.

'Most of them appear to be consultation services. And they all link back to a construction company in the United Kingdom – a company called Clover Shore Construction. They didn't found the company, but their skill at hiding paper trails and lines of income has been invaluable to the people that run it. Recently, however, they have rather upset their employers by siphoning off money into secret accounts. They should have known better. Their employers have decided it would be best if they conveniently…disappeared.'

I felt I was being too silent and became aware of Argento looking at me, as if he was expecting me to contribute in some way. I opened my mouth, and when I did speak, my voice was cracked and rough, as if I'd been asleep for a very long time. 'What…um…what does Clover Shore Construction do?'

'They provide products and services upon request. They provide people with the things they desire, and the environments in which they can…encounter such desires.'

'Environments?' you asked.

Perhaps the question upset him or he didn't want Argento to continue, but for whatever reason, the male in the cage seemed to become distressed or agitated. He began to writhe, causing the chains that held him to clink and shake. The one around his neck made its unpleasant scraping sound on the wall, and he began to moan, but the sound was muffled and inaudible.

'I don't think Mr Greene here wants you to know the answer to that question,' Argento said, grinning. The movement seemed to have woken his wife, and she too started to jerk and look around her. 'Isn't it interesting that when the boot is on the other foot, so to speak, people like him always seem to develop a sense of shame? A conscience? I wonder how much of it is real, and how much of it is a survival mechanism.'

I stared at the figures crouched on the stone floor. I wondered if I should be feeling pity, but all I could muster up was a dull sense of unease. Greater still was my sense of suspense. I wanted Argento to continue. I wanted to find out more.

From the end of the room, Argento went to a shelf that was mostly empty aside from a small row of books, folders and video cassettes in cardboard sleeves. He picked up a folder, dusted it with his hand lightly even though it looked pristine, and opened it up. He took two sheets from inside. He handed one to you and one to me.

It's strange what ends up staying in one's mind. The contents of that sheet of paper would haunt me from that moment on, for the rest of my life. Even after everything I would actually see, it's odd how a page of printed text can sear itself into one's mind even more effectively than the most horrifying of images.

Once I'd read it through, I looked up to see Argento staring at me. 'You understand what it is?'

I nodded.

'It's a product listing,' you said.

'Correct,' Argento said, turning to you, looking impressed.

Both Mr and Mrs Greene in the cage behind him started to writhe again.

I looked down at the sheet once more. At the different categories. Name. Location. Age. And 'activities available'. *Activities*.

'These pieces of paper are part of a catalogue only clients of Clover Field Construction are normally allowed to see. There are hundreds of pages. And of course, when one of the 'products' has served its purpose, the pages are destroyed. From what I understand, a lot of the products don't live long.'

Argento then turned and walked towards the door at the end. I knew what was coming before he wheeled it into view. Just like last time, he was going to show us a film.

'This is where things get very interesting. This is something Mrs Greene here doesn't know.' He kicked the cage again, causing her to flinch and clasp her husband's hand tighter.

'Let me see…ah, here we are.' Argento selected a video from the shelf and inserted it into a machine. 'My sources tell me this was covertly recorded in a deserted and abandoned multi-storey car park in Rainham, East London.'

From what I could see from the fuzzy footage, a group of men were standing around in a circle, with a small car in the centre. And leaning up against the car were two shapes. Moving.

'Oh my God,' I said, without thinking.

'I know,' Argento said, 'it's disturbing to witness, isn't it? The young man participating in that spectacle is actually the son of a British Member of Parliament. But perhaps we'll save that story for another day. The person I want to show you is about to come into view.'

Another man, one of the observers, walked into full view.

'This,' Argento said, 'Is Mr Greene.'

We watched in horror as Harry started to participate. Or at least, I presumed that you shared my horror. But when I glanced at you, just once, your face was impassive and you didn't look back at me. Just stared at the screen.

'The interesting thing about this,' Argento continued, 'is that I believe Mrs Greene here did not know that Mr Greene enjoyed sampling the human products the catalogue offered.'

I looked over at the cage. The woman was starting to move. Straining against her chains, she had released her husband's hand and was now moving away from him, tears in her eyes.

'But we should not let Mrs Greene off the hook. She has been instrumental in making the business grow. A business that had been going for a number of decades in a smaller, more exclusive sort of way. But Mrs Greene helped make it global.'

'Turn off the tape,' I said.

Argento raised his eyebrows. 'Is the content too strong for you, Oliver?' he asked. 'Or…is this perhaps impatience? You want me to progress to the next step?' He didn't wait for an answer. 'Very well.' He paused the video. The nightmarish scene on the screen paused and jerked and flickered. I swallowed and took a deep breath.

I expected Argento to take out the snakeskin case like last time, but instead, he went back through the door at the end of the room once again and returned wheeling another object. It looked like a workman's table, but on wheels. A rough wooden countertop, with items laid out upon it.

I had managed to stay calm up until this point. Managed not to panic, not run away, not bail out from what we were doing. But seeing what was on that table was the hardest test so far.

'As you can see, their outer clothing has been removed to allow you the broadest possible of canvasses,' Argento said as he brought the bench to a stop in front of us. 'I invite you both to be…creative…in the justice you want them both to feel.'

On its surface was a collection of tools. A hammer. A kitchen knife. A staple-gun. Some pliers. A blow torch.

Even though the sound was dull and muffled under their gags, I could tell they were trying to scream in desperation.

I look up at him. Then over at you. I expected – hoped – your face would reflect my horror at what was being offered to us. But I saw no such horror in your face. You looked completely calm. Completely unfazed. And, worst of all, in that moment, you slowly reached out a hand. You settled it gently on the blow torch. Then you picked it up.

'An interesting choice, Alastair,' Argento said. 'Oliver, do you have a weapon of choice?'

I felt nauseated by the question. 'I…no.'

Once again, Argento raised an eyebrow. 'Are you sure?'

I looked back at the table of tools. 'Is there…can't we…can't you…the syringe?'

Argento looked at me for a few seconds, then smiled. 'Of course.' He produced from his pocket the snakeskin wallet. As soon as he did so, you put down the blow torch.

'I think,' you said, quietly, 'what Oliver is saying is that we're more here to…well, watch, rather than participate.'

Argento's smile decreased somewhat. Then he nodded. 'I understand. Of course, we'll proceed in whatever way you feel comfortable. You are my guests, after all.'

He set down the wallet and took out the vial of clear liquid and the syringe. 'Come closer, though,' he said, as he pushed the syringe into the top of the vial. 'You'll want a better view.'

Chapter Twenty-Six

NOW

'When did it start?' you ask, watching me closely, your head turned to the side on your lounger by the pool. 'Your problems with addiction? Was it to do with…what we did?'

I tell you about the pills. About the pain. The pain nobody could find any reason for. Even though I knew, deep down, what the reason had to be.

I feel something tighten in my chest as I answer.

'I'm…not sure. There were a few things that happened, after I left Greece. I went home to England for a while, but ended up postponing my masters for a year. I think my mind just wasn't in the right space for it. So I travelled. Went to Munich in the autumn, followed by Berlin in December. I met Douglas there for the week leading up to Christmas, then we both flew back on the twenty-second of December. On the flight, or rather the lead-up to it, something odd happened to me. Douglas and I were walking across the tarmac to the plane and I felt this…I don't know how to describe it. This…weight.

A strange weight inside me. Pulling me down. Like I could barely move. I think Douglas just thought I was battling against the cold wind and snow that was starting to come down – it was being blown into our faces as we moved towards the plane. But I just had this horrible sense of dread. Really, terrible dread. The sky was grey, it was near twilight, and all of a sudden everything around me felt like it was… well, evil. Like there was something terrible lurking behind the dark clouds, something that at any second would see me and know…know what I had done. As I got to the stairs up to the aircraft, I heard it…'

'It?' you ask, frowning.

'The crash. A motorway runs round alongside the terminal near the airport. There was a crash – a huge crash, a multiple pile-up. And then an explosion. People were shouting. We could see the flames, even though the cars were too far away to make out. As I turned to look at the chaos, I lost my footing and fell down the first few steps onto the tarmac. Hurt my shoulder.' I feel my hand go to touch it, as if my whole arm were on a string and someone else was lifting it for me. When I realise what I am doing I drop it to my side.

'You were injured?'

'No,' I reply, quietly. 'Well, some minor jarring, but there wasn't actually any specific injury. But the pain was insane. I fainted and woke up in a medical room at the airport with my brother crouching over me, trying to get me to drink some water. But I didn't really see him. I mean, I could see him, but it was like looking through a TV screen, as though something was playing out on the image behind him.'

'What was it?'

My breath shudders as I draw it in then let it out. 'The crash. It was as though I could see the crash that had happened on the motorway, probably half a mile away. As though I could hear the screams of the people, trapped in crashed cars. Dying from bleeding wounds. I could...*feel* them. There's no other way to describe it.'

A slight frown creases your brow for the first time since you arrived. 'I imagine you'd hit your head from the fall. Or were just in shock.'

'That would be the rational explanation,' I say. And I know how tempting that explanation would be to go with. I'd tried to convince myself it was true, often enough, over the past twenty years.

'And what would be the irrational explanation?' you ask.

'That it wasn't the people in the crash I was hearing.'

You say nothing. Waiting.

'That it was them. All the people we killed.'

You raise an eyebrow. 'I thought we didn't kill anyone? I thought it was all about watching.'

Now it's my turn to say nothing. Eventually, you ask another question. 'Is there a particular person that you think about the most? Out of all the people we ended up seeing killed, is there one that you always return to?'

It takes me so long to speak, I'm surprised you don't prompt me. At last, I manage to get my words out, though they're not words I want to say.

'Sometimes I wonder how we managed to keep returning to the island, knowing we were going to witness another killing. I know *why* I went. Or at least, one of the reasons. I just don't know...in those early days, when death was such an unknown thing. I don't know how we could have done that, over and over.'

You move, smoothly but quickly, lifting yourself up onto your elbows and swinging your legs over the lounger so they rest on the floor. Sitting on the edge, facing me directly, you talk quietly: 'Oliver, I'm sorry to be blunt, but you're trying to look closer at this than you need to. It was entertainment, that's all. Human beings are naturally drawn to both the light and the dark. We just spent some time in the dark. It's not saying it's *right*, but there's no mystery to it. Not that aspect, anyway. And because it wasn't us pulling the trigger, so to speak, it was easy to return for more.' You let these words hit home for a moment, then ask, 'Did you ever wonder what it would have been like if *you* had chosen to kill someone? Had chosen not to be a passive participant, but an active one?'

I know this is now or never. If I don't say what I have to say now, I never will. I take a deep breath, then reply. 'I did exactly that. That's why I thought you were dead. I thought I had killed you.'

Chapter Twenty-Seven

THEN

We'd been going to the island every week for 'the sessions' as we began to call them. It felt astonishing to me that we could talk of something so huge – experiences so huge – as if we were popping out for a gig or a game of tennis. But there was something delicious in that. Delicious in the fact that we were stepping so far out of society's lines of what was acceptable without having to answer for it. I think it probably gave us a godlike feeling, being able to observe from a safe distance something as momentous as the extinguishing of life.

On the last weekend of August, I started to have a feeling of concern. I knew our lives couldn't continue the way they were. Very soon, you and I would have to cross the great silence that has built up between us. I occasionally offered wild suggestions, of us building palaces together, or joining circuses, or becoming librarians together at one of the Greek universities. Anything to put off the cold hard reality: autumn was fast approaching. At the end of September, I was supposed to be flying back with my family to England and to start my

MA in Durham. That was a plan made in the past, before I knew my true self. Before you. Before Argento.

In the end, I didn't have to make a decision. At least, not about all that specifically. A decision was made – the most difficult I had ever had to face. It at least solved a number of dilemmas in quick succession. But the price I had to pay was terrible. Truly terrible.

Leaving the hostel dorm that evening felt odd. The sun was lower than usual – a sure sign the season was changing – letting in a rich golden light that fell across our beds. Something about it made me linger for a moment. 'Ready?' you asked, looking over at me from the doorway. There wasn't any reason to pause, and yet that's exactly what I did, like a schoolboy on the front step who was worried he'd forgotten his homework. But there was nothing I needed to remember, nothing I needed to bring. We never took anything over to the island. We didn't bother with swimming things or towels. Part of me had wondered if perhaps Argento liked the image of two strapping young men padding about dripping wet, our white briefs rendered translucent by the pool water. I'd never examined whether there was a sexual element to our host's fascination with us. Or if it was just about power.

We journeyed over to the island on that late-summer weekend with a strange atmosphere between us, the uneasy feeling I'd had when leaving the dorm remaining around me, like a cloak I couldn't shrug off. It was as if we both knew it would be our last trip – as if we knew something would happen during that 'session' that would change the course of our future. I didn't have much time for concepts of sixth sense or second sight. But then again, there was a time when I wouldn't have had much time for being an accessory to multiple murders. People can change, it seems.

During the boat trip, perhaps to gain some control over the strange feeling that had gripped me, I turned to you, taking hold of your arm. I told you it was a mark of our sense of compatibility, closeness and commitment, the fact that we'd found each other: two souls who were willing to confront the darkness of human nature and face up to what it is they liked. You said nothing for a while, staring over the side at the rippling water. Then you just replied with typical simplicity, 'I agree.'

When we got to the island, Argento greeted us with his usual relaxed smile. 'We are to dine in reverse, today,' he said, then explained that he had set up a buffet of fruit and extremely expensive chocolates by the swimming pool. We were to swim and enjoy the food as a sort of dessert-starter. Then we would get dry, he said, and have our savoury course on the veranda with him and today's guest.

The evening played out just as he had described. The fruit was delicious, mounds of it collected on plates dotted around the pool area – too much for the two of us to consume. You became very enthusiastic about some praline truffles with a cashew-flavoured coating and insisted we brought the tray of them to the poolside so we could enjoy them whilst swimming.

'You're not supposed to eat whilst swimming,' I playfully reprimanded him. 'It'll make you feel sick. And you can get cramp.'

You grinned at me, wickedly, biting down on the hard shell of one of the chocolates. 'That's not true,' you said. 'It's a myth.' You then came over to me and wrapped your arms around my shoulders. I was about to tell you I really didn't think the part about sickness was a myth, but then you were kissing me, allowing the slightly molten chocolate in your mouth to slide into mine. The combination of your tongue and the sweetness of the truffle was truly divine and made me breathless. I drew away, telling you that we shouldn't get so excited, not here.

'We shouldn't do it here,' I whispered, as your hands started to move down beneath the water.

You just laughed quietly, a sound that was both deep and light at the same time, and then you were guiding me over to the side, your mouth on mine again. I couldn't deny you what you wanted. I never could, not back then. The feeling of your chest meeting the flesh of my back reminded me of our first time together. That intoxicating night when everything had changed. Just a matter of weeks in the past, and yet it felt like a million years ago.

We had barely time to get our breath back when we heard someone speak to our left.

'Now that you are finished with your exertions,' Argento said, amusement in his voice, 'it is time to get dry and join us over on the veranda for the main course.'

We dried off quickly, dressed and followed Argento round to the veranda to find a white-haired old man in a wheelchair. He was introduced to us as Sir Hector. His presence disturbed me. Was this old man really to be our 'subject' for the evening? Was he to be drugged and wake up, stripped and frightened, in one of the cells below us? I hadn't had the same concern for any of our past guests, but they had all been adults aged between thirty and fifty. It had, in some way, managed to separate 'them' from 'us', rendering the subjects as 'other'. It was easier that way. For some reason, though, it felt different contemplating such things with someone so old. Perhaps it was their proximity to death already, as if we were interrupting a natural process that would befall him whether we intervened or not.

'Ah, you've found them,' Sir Hector said, beaming from his seat at the table. He sounded English, with an instantly warm, welcoming tone. 'Come, join me, boys. Our host is just busy selecting the candle for the evening.'

Sure enough, as we were taking our seats, Argento returned from a side table to his left holding a large but flat-looking terracotta pot and set it in the centre of the table, which was filled with dishes of cured meats and cheeses. 'This is a special scented candle I had shipped over from Iran. It has notes of saffron, rose and smoked wood. It reminds me of my time travelling the Persian markets during my twenties.'

As the candle was lit, I realised this was the first time Argento had spoken about something specific in his younger years. He had alluded to experiences, but never anything as concrete as this. I felt a chink of the real man had been revealed, and I wasn't sure I liked it. Perhaps the only way I could deal with the island and what happened upon it was to consider him and his way of life a mystery, an enigma, a puzzle that should never be solved.

The candle was as evocative as advertised, its smoky, woody notes making me feel light-headed and a little sleepy.

Sir Hector and Argento spent the majority of our meal discussing art. You chatted to him politely about your own degree, but as ever you didn't give much away of your past, or indeed of your opinions. In spite of this, I had the strange sense Sir Hector already knew who you were. A rogue thought floated into my mind. A note of concern and danger, that perhaps, at some point, we would be having dinner not with our next 'subject', but with our murderer. That we would become the prey, to wake up in the cages, with Sir Hector being wheeled in to observe or participate in our deaths. I tried to dismiss this image and watched as you spoke about how your father used to be an art collector and before he died he'd opened a gallery called Halcyon. I noticed Sir Hector's eyes switch to Argento for a moment at this mention of your father, then return to you. It struck me as odd at the time, but I became distracted when he then fixed his beetle-black eyes on me.

'And what about you, Oliver?' he asked kindly.

'Oh…I…well…I studied English at Durham. I'm returning there to do a Masters in the autumn.'

He nodded and made some brief reference to a particular church in Durham he was particularly fond of.

I spent most of the meal zoning out, my thoughts becoming slow, like they were made of a thick, glutinous substance, or even heavy snow, packed in tight around the edges of my brain.

'Oliver.'

I became vaguely aware someone was speaking to me. And for a second, I could have sworn Nita was standing there in front of me. Saying my name. A wound on her neck. Clear liquid running out of it, like water from a fountain.

'Oliver.'

It wasn't Nita, of course. It was you. 'I was just telling Sir Hector about the art project we've agreed to take part in. With Argento.'

I looked at him in confusion, then over at Sir Hector, who was smiling calmly at me. 'I understand young Alastair here has quite a considerable collection. I'm only sad I won't be able to enjoy it. I think it's unlikely I'll be visiting the mainland again.'

'Oh,' I said, because I wasn't sure what else to say. I looked over at you and immediately you came to my rescue. 'I'm going to loan some of my father's collection of Albert Bierstadt paintings. Argento would like us to help him set up an exhibition at a gallery in Athens.'

'Right,' I said, nodding slowly.

'That's if there's enough interest in Bierstadt these days,' Sir Hector said, tilting a flat hand a little, as if to suggest he doubted it.

It was clear to me there was subtext going on here. And the slightest chill spread across the back of my neck when Argento caught my eye.

There was no project, or at least not one that you cared about. I could see all this for what it was: foreplay.

Eventually. we reached a point in the evening when Argento turned his eyes upon me and rose from his seat. He didn't speak, but instead mouthed the words 'Come with me.'

Sir Hector had you in conversation, although I saw your eyes flick over to me as I stood. I laid a gentle hand on your shoulder as I left the table as a way of saying, 'Back in a moment.'

Part of me expected Argento to lead me down the side of the villa to the steps leading to the dungeon. But instead he just walked straight into the villa and along its main hallway, then took a right, down another dimly lit corridor. There was a room at the end, the door slightly ajar.

'Go inside,' Argento said, standing back to allow me through.

I hesitated, fearful of what I was about to witness. Or experience. From my time visiting the island, I'd learned that anything was possible.

The room beyond the door was a bedroom – large, but simply furnished, with a kingsize bed in the centre, a small table holding a jug of what appeared to be water, and an ornately upholstered chair to its left. I turned to look back at Argento, and as I did so I noticed another table near the wall. This one held a television, identical to the one we'd seen many times in the dungeon.

Argento walked over to the bed and laid a hand on the pristine cream-white covers. 'It was on this bed where Nita had one of her last experiences before she made the transition from life to death.'

I realised what he was referring to. 'Yes. I'm aware my brother had sex with Nita before she…she made that transition.' I decided it would be best to adopt the language Argento used instead of using blunt, potentially accusatory language such as 'before you killed her'.

Argento nodded and a smile began to spread over his face. 'I'm sorry to tell you this, Oliver, as I suspect the news will not be to your liking, but the last man Nita gave herself to wasn't Douglas. It was Alastair.'

I felt my perception of the temperature around me change. The warm room had suddenly become cold. 'No...no that's not...*Douglas* had sex with Nita. It wasn't...' My mind was looping back to that night, when we had sat on my bed, when you told me what had happened that evening on the island. It couldn't be true. You wouldn't be that dishonest with me. It wasn't possible.

'Turn around and face the television, Oliver,' Argento said, calmly.

With a terrible, rising dread within me, I obeyed.

Argento turned the set on. Then heard the click as the built-in VCR player started up. Then the image arrived on the screen.

Fuzzy black-and-white, but it was still very clear as to what was going on. The footage was of this room. And on the bed were two people having sex. Nita was on all fours on the bed and a male figure was enthusiastically thrusting into her from behind. And for a moment, I experienced a rush of relief. This form was much taller and more muscular than you were. Then he raised his head and I saw his face properly. It was Douglas. I had no wish to see my brother in the midst of such an activity, but I was so pleased to see it was him and not...

There was someone else. Lingering at the edge of the image. Unidentifiable. Waiting.

Douglas was going at it very fast and a sudden end to his movements, his head going back, suggested he'd climaxed. He flopped down onto the bed for a bit, apparently catching his breath, then he got up. He seemed to be smiling and laughing, saying something to someone – the person just visible at the edge of the frame. It was impossible to tell what was being said. There was no sound to the footage. He laughed again, then moved out of shot. And then the unidentified presence walked on into the frame. And it was clear who it was.

'No...' I said, crouching down in front of the screen, watching as you become fully visible, clearly identifiable. Unlike Douglas, you were fully dressed, in shorts, shirt and sandals. Even on the monochrome footage I could tell you were wearing the red shirt I loved so much. The red shirt you'd been wearing when I first met you. The shirt you had been wearing that night you came to the island without me. Nita had moved herself to the edge of the bed and changed position, lying on her back, her legs parted. You didn't even have to get on the bed to do what you did next. You just kicked off your sandals, tugged down your shorts and spent the following five minutes of footage destroying my world. I could barely watch. I could barely see. It was a while before I realised it wasn't the video that had become blurry, it was the tears filling my eyes and falling down my face.

I was in the grip of shock. Sadness. Fury. The world as I knew it was being reshaped before my very eyes – and, worse than that, it had all happened weeks ago. Over a month ago. I had been living through a lie without knowing it since that time, believing you and I were two kindred spirits, committed to nobody but each other, fellow travellers through this strange world, ready to experience and share its dark delights in ways we could only find in each other. And aside from the betrayal, there was another question: how could you have so calmly had sex with this woman and then observed her murder?

We had spent the whole summer convincing ourselves we weren't monsters. Suddenly I was wondering how we had got everything so very, very wrong.

The words Douglas had spoken to me, just before he'd departed Greece, came back to me in that moment. *Just be careful, Oliver…I'm worried you're going to get hurt…*

This was the hurt he was referring to. He knew you had fucked Nita straight after him that night. He had even laughed and joked with you. I felt another pang of hurt hit me. Hurt that Douglas could have kept this from me. His vague warnings could not excuse this. He knew how much I cared for you. Perhaps that was part of the reason he had fled Greece. Perhaps the guilt of being part of this secret was too much for him.

'As I said, I'm sorry to cause you pain by showing you this,' Argento said, his voice making me start. I'd almost forgotten he was there at all. I'd been swallowed up so totally by the nightmare unfolding on the screen, everything else had disappeared into darkness around me.

'How could he…' I said in a half-whisper, 'How could he watch her die just after doing this?' I turned to look at Argento, desperate for answers.

And as I asked, I think I realised the answers wouldn't be ones I wanted to hear.

'Alastair didn't watch her death,' Argento said, still in his slow, calm voice. 'He killed her.'

All I could do was stare at him.

'Come, Oliver. I have more to show you.'

Chapter Twenty-Eight

THEN

A rgento led me down a short walk along a corridor leading away from the bedroom and then down a set of three steps. It opened out onto a kitchen area – quite large, with a dark wooden table taking up most of its space.

'As we have done before, I thought we could all enjoy some coffee after our meal. Thick and black. The best way to consume it, in my view.'

My head was hurting after the sudden surge of anguish and disorientation I'd felt in the bedroom. I couldn't understand why I'd been shown in here, to where our coffee was being made. Why Argento was moving the mugs towards me so that they were right in front of me on the table in a neat line.

'I am going to leave you here alone, Oliver. I think you need some time by yourself to make sense of what you have seen tonight. And while you allow your mind to take in all that you have discovered – all that you now know – I'd like you to make a decision.'

He brought something out from his pocket.

And that's when I understood what was going on here.

That's when I understood what was being asked of me.

The decision that would be left in my hands.

Argento unzipped the snakeskin wallet and took out the familiar vial of clear liquid.

'I'm giving you a very important opportunity, Oliver. The opportunity to choose who you would like to remove from this life,' he said. 'You could decide to remove the person you thought was your one true love, who has lied to you and cheated on you. Or you could choose to remove an elderly man who is close to death, terminally ill with cancer. An elderly man who has committed his fair share of sins, I promise you. Or you could choose to remove *me* – the man who has shaken your world. I have, as gently as I could, threatened your family. Blackmailed you, essentially. Forced you into coming back here, because I sensed you needed that *push*. Or you could choose to leave this life yourself. Or, last but certainly not least, you have the choice to leave our coffees untouched and keep things exactly the way they are.'

I felt as if the room was swaying. I hadn't experienced anything like this level of inner torment since I'd witnessed that first session – that first killing – back at the start of the summer. When I'd chosen to stay and watched the life leave Jax Wolf's eyes.

Could I do that to another human being? Could I make that journey, cross that magnificent gulf, close the gap of difference between silent accomplice and active participant?

Murderer.

Then my mind offered up an image. An image I wished I

had never seen. An image of you and Nita. The grey, grainy nature of the footage I'd watched adding to the nightmarish quality of the scenes I'd sat through. Scenes that had killed something inside of me.

You would deserve it, I thought to myself. The thought shocked me only for a moment, then it landed comfortably within me, like a puzzle piece slotting into place. I think that was when I knew I had what it took to be able to do what I needed to do. Make that leap. Become a killer. Because in that moment, nobody in this world could be worse than you. Nobody could possibly have committed worse crimes.

But as I reached out my hand, ready to take the vial, something made me stop. I paused for a few seconds, doing nothing, just staring at the coffee mugs. Then I looked up at Argento and asked him a question that had just arrived in my mind.

'What crimes has Sir Hector committed?'

Argento looked slightly surprised for a moment, then his calm smile returned. He set the vial down on the counter top. 'You want to see how the scales balance? I respect that, Oliver. I really do. So I shall tell you. There are many possible beginnings to this remarkable tale. Can I ask, have you heard of the small village in the Essex countryside known as Tolleshunt D'Arcy?'

I frowned. 'I don't think so.'

'Well, I have a lot to tell you. Let us take a seat.'

And so instead of leaving me, my great decision was postponed for a further ten minutes. Argento took his time to carefully tell me his story. Or rather Sir Hector's story. Of what he had done. The lives he had ruined because of his actions, because of the obsession he had for a particular person. The far-reaching consequences – ripples that were sent across different people, different families, different continents, spanning the small English village he mentioned all the way to the United States of America. The story astonished me. It was like nothing I'd ever heard, like a novel playing out before me, Argento's deep, impactful voice making the telling of it quite extraordinary. When Argento stood, I stayed seated, staring at the mugs before me.

'And now I really must leave you. For one of our guests, it will likely be his last night on this earth. It would be a shame for that night to be marred by a less-than-attentive host. Don't take too long in your deliberations, Oliver. Make a choice, based on what you've heard, then bring us our coffee. ' He gestured to the whirring machine behind him, then nodded again to the four mugs in front of me. 'I shall be waiting for you.'

The setting sun bathed the room in cold light, shining in from the window behind me. The glasses on the table glinted. The smooth polished surfaces gleamed and then, as the sun continued its downward descent, started to dim.

I couldn't stay here too long, I told myself. I needed to decide. I knew whatever choice I made wouldn't just affect the person who died. It would change me too. I'd already gone through so much, seen so much. Everything that had happened over that summer felt like it had led me to that moment. The moment I truly held the powers of life and death in my hands.

In the end, I had to take a look. I stepped out into the open hallway that led to the veranda. I could see my three choices before me. The person who had brought me here. An elderly man who was at the end of his life. Or you. You, who had occupied my thoughts, reshaped my existence and stolen my heart.

One death would solve a major problem. Remove the man who had a hold over my family. Another could be excused as a kindness, offering a dying man a quiet, painless exit. And the third would be revenge.

I could have stayed there for hours. Deliberating. Considering my options. Putting off making my decision. But I decided to put a stop to it.

I made my choice.

I poured out the coffees and placed them on the tray. Then I opened the small vial of clear liquid.

I carried them carefully back out to the outdoor seating area.

Argento locked eyes with me as I laid the tray down and gave me a short nod. I looked down at the mugs, my hand hovering over them. I could feel the steam coating my hand as it stayed there, suspended.

'Are you OK?' you asked. I looked over at you and found that it was easy to smile.

'I'm fine,' I said. And then handed you a coffee.

I entered a new phase of my life that night. A phase of horror. Something that gouged deep into me. Phrases like 'soul' had always made me uncomfortable. But from that moment, I knew they existed. And I knew mine had been twisted. Damaged. Made ugly. Perhaps it had happened a long while ago. I stared into the water on the way back to the mainland. I didn't speak once to the man steering the boat, and he didn't talk to me. He didn't ask why I was, for the first time ever, making this crossing alone.

I stayed in the centre of the boat, only going to the side once, in order to let go over the side the one item I was carrying. The thing Argento had given to me, when everything was over, almost as a prize. A video cassette. A tape I never wanted to see again. I let it fall into the waves without hesitation.

Blue sapphire darkness surrounded me. The lights in the hostel foyer burned. I didn't know if I was wise to return there without you. But it was closer than my family villa, and I knew I couldn't face them. Not at that moment. Not after what had happened. I just needed to sleep.

I went over to your bed when I reached the dormitory, but found I was unable to get into it. I touched the sheets, briefly raising them to my face, then dropping them as if scalded, and turned to the bed nearest. There I lay down and tried to fall asleep, lying to myself that things would be better when I woke. It was a lie I wasn't able to believe as I tried not to imagine your voice, telling me to join you, inviting me to fall into your arms, your hands, the warm feel of your flesh keeping me safe. The room was dark, empty and, for the first time, felt cold. I pulled the sheets around me and slept.

When I woke, there was someone else in the room, and dimly, for a few seconds – a few, wonderful, hopeful seconds – I felt the relief you get after waking from a nightmare. Only this relief was tragically short-lived.

'Hey, man, which bed should I take, because that one's kind of a mess. Is someone else sleeping here too?'

I looked at the person in front of me – a short-ish, skinny guy with brown hair and glasses. He had an American accent and a T-shirt with a picture of a marijuana leaf on it. 'Oh... sorry, what?'

'I've just arrived. Staying here for a week. How long you here for? Girl at the desk didn't mention how many others were here. Although I guess she was too caught up in the news.'

With an immense effort, I got up, dressed quickly and left the room. I think the new arrival called something out, possibly 'Bye', but I didn't say anything. I just hurried down the stairs and into the reception.

The young woman at the desk was crying. The sight of it disconcerted me. I immediately froze in front of the scuffed counter-top. It was a moment before I realised the TV was on. She clearly seemed to think I'd know what she was crying about, because she pointed at the TV screen to her right and asked if I wanted to watch it too. I told her I didn't understand. She just shook her head and muttered something. 'So sad,' I think. Something like that. Then started dabbing at her eyes with a frayed tissue.

I knew then, watching that news report unfold, that my life from then on would be a thousand times harder than I could possibly have imagined. Because there was no way I'd ever be able to forget this day. And nobody else would forget it either. It would be seared into the history books. Every year it would come round, and people would remember. The last day of

August, 1997. The last day of a summer that would change the world.

'I saw her once,' the crying girl said. 'When I was living in England, she came to the hospital I was staying in. All the staff were really excited. The princess coming to visit. I had appendicitis, but had been discharged and was on my way out. But she still smiled at me. Even though I wasn't really sick.' Quietly, she continued to sob.

I was shocked. Appalled. But I needed to go. 'Sorry,' I said, 'I'll leave you to it.'

She turned to look at me, blinking through her tears. 'What? Hey, are you booked in here—'

I ignored this last bit, cursing myself for drawing attention to my presence after all this time, on this day when it could have been vital for me to slip out unnoticed. My eyes protesting at the harsh light of the sun outside, I began to make my way to my family's villa.

By the time I'd reached it and had stepped through the front door, I knew what I wanted. I knew what I needed. I needed to get out of Greece. To go home. To put as much distance as possible, in miles and thought, between this place and myself. I also knew such a request wasn't going to be easy, but I was so determined I would have flown home alone if I'd had to.

When I got inside, I heard my mother and father talking in the lounge. My mother was crying, and for one terrible moment I thought they both knew; knew what I had done, knew what their son had become. Knew of my shame.

But it was the news Mum was crying about. She was

crouched in front of the TV screen, her hand outstretched, as though she might be able to touch the woman's face that filled it. It was clearly another news report, the announcer speaking Greek, his words drowned out by my father who said grumpily, 'I told you, I tried to get the English language news channel and it won't work, it doesn't matter how much you sob and complain!'

He stopped when he saw me come in. 'Oh, it's you. Have you heard the news?'

I didn't get a chance to reply before my mother stood up and rushed over to me. 'Oliver, darling, *darling*, isn't it dreadful?' She pulled me into a hug and sobbed into my shoulder. 'I should have seen it. The horoscopes would have warned me of this, if only I'd read them properly.'

'Mum, stop,' I said, trying to pull away from her.

'Has it upset you? We should call some people. We didn't know the family, but we must have friends who did.'

'Just stop!' I shouted the words, making both my parents stand completely still, looking at me. 'I think we should leave Greece. Today.'

As soon as I said it, I felt a sense of relief. Nothing had been solved, nothing was certain, but I knew it was what I needed to do.

My mother looked aghast. 'What? Why? Because of all this?' She gestured to the TV, but I shook my head.

'No, I just…just want to go home.'

'What are you talking about?' said Dad gruffly. 'Gosh, first your brother, now you. I'm tired of the pair of you. All this doesn't come cheap, you know. I pay a fortune for it all and it ends up being hell on earth.'

I saw the hurt on my mother's face, 'Oh well, if it's *hell on earth,* maybe we should leave,' she said dramatically. 'I'll just have to accept that the whole summer has been a disaster, with Douglas storming off and everyone being simply horrid.'

Dad turned his back on my mum and eyed me suspiciously. 'There's something you're not telling us. What's caused this?'

I didn't have the energy. I turned to go out of the room, but my father followed me.

'You can't just come in here, throw a grenade like that into the room and wander off. Tell us why we need to go home.'

Halfway up the stairs I paused. Then slowly I turned and forced myself to talk as calmly and clearly as I could. 'I saw your friend Argento last night. He said to tell you he's coming here today. Has something to show you, apparently.'

I knew the effect the lie would likely have on him. I watched as he grew pale, his eyes locked on mine. I held his gaze. Then my father slowly nodded and said in a quieter, much smaller voice, 'I think it would be a good idea for us to leave Greece today.'

Chapter Twenty-Nine

NOW

'I knew I had been drugged,' you say, 'but I presumed at the time it was one of Argento's games.'

I raise my eyebrows. 'You...he didn't tell you...you didn't think I...'

'I'll get to that,' you say, a little curtly.

'Sorry,' I say, then wonder why I'm bothering to apologise. But I know why. Even after everything, I still want to please you. Keep you talking to me. My first instinct is to be guided by you. An instinct that I picked up quickly when we first met and that, it seems, has never left me since.

'When I woke up,' you continue, 'I was alone and he – Argento – said that Sir Hector had died, and you'd gone back to the mainland. That you'd seen...footage of me and Nita...together.'

I feel a pang of something in my chest. The ghost of the hurt and sadness I'd initially felt at that time.

'I didn't blame you. For leaving me, that is.'

But not for trying to kill him. The words remain unspoken, but I know what you're saying. Part of me is intrigued to know if Argento ever told you the full story, if you'd been sitting with me here the whole time, all these years later, aware of everything I'd done.

'I sat at that table watching you starting to grow drowsy,' I say, quietly. 'I was convinced you were dying. And…'

'And,' you prompt, after a few moments, sounding surprisingly gentle.

'And the worst thing about it,' I say, wiping a stray tear away, 'was that I didn't mean to kill you. I had decided to kill Sir Hector. I thought that it was a test. A test Argento was setting for me. I decided that Sir Hector was the natural choice. An old man who would be dead soon anyway. It was like a mercy killing.' I raise my eyes to you, and you can see the pleading in my face.

'I understand,' you say, quietly.

I take a shuddering breath, then continue. 'But when I put the tray down on the table I panicked and suddenly doubted which cup was which. I should have just gone back into the villa, or thrown the tray on the ground and pretend I'd dropped it. But I was scared what would happen, scared Argento would come up with something else, something nastier, follow through on…well, on certain threats he'd made. What he said about Douglas, of course, and the used condoms. Plus some other things too. And…this is going to sound weird, but…I didn't want him to think I'd failed the challenge. He had this way of making me feel like I was constantly being assessed for higher status. So when I saw you starting to fall asleep, I thought I'd given you the spiked one. Turns out, I'd given the correct one to Sir Hector all along.'

You nod. Lower your gaze to the floor for a bit. Then you say, 'Well, I guess that means we're both murderers. In the end, we both made that jump.'

I don't know what I expected you to say. I'm still putting all the pieces of this story together, my mind tangled and stretched. 'So now we know we're the same,' I say slowly, 'where does that leave us?'

You look as though you're making a decision about something. When you do speak, you look me straight in the eye. And there's a glint there now. Something new. Something resembling excitement. 'That leaves you with potentially helping me with something. Something for old times' sake. But first, I think we should go back to your room.'

Chapter Thirty

NOW

We don't bother getting dressed to go back to my room. We just take two hotel-branded bathrobes from the changing rooms and carry the rest of our things. I think we both know what's going to happen, even though we don't say it to each other. This is the language we know, the language of lust and passion, the unspoken actions that we became experts in.

Once inside my room, you instantly reach for the back of my neck, your hand grasping it as you pull me into a deep, long kiss. Within seconds, our bathrobes are discarded on the floor, our hands moving around each other's bodies. Then we're on the bed. It's rough, desperate, animalistic, just like it used to be on those hot Greek nights, and within our movements and gasps is over twenty years of loss and longing, pent-up anger and desire and love.

Afterwards, you roll off me, and we lie on the bed, breathless and dazed, the half-open curtains only letting in a shallow grey late-autumn gloom. You don't speak, so neither do I, and into my mind flits words I had not long ago read – words by the author Daniel Mendelsohn, on how, during the act of gay sex, men *'fall through their partners back into themselves, over and over again'*. This prompts me to reach for my phone to look up the passage online.

'What are you doing?' you ask, dully, your face in the pillow.

I find the extract on Google Books and begin to read out loud: *'I have had sex with many men. Most of them look a certain way. They are medium in height and tend to prettiness. They will probably have blue eyes. They seem, from the street, or across the room, a bit solemn. When I hold them, it is like falling through a reflection back into my desire, into the thing that defines me, my self.'*

You let a few beats of silence pass, then say, 'What is that?'

'It's just something I read recently. I wanted to look at it again.'

'You thought I'd want to hear that?'

I lock my phone and roll onto my side towards you. Our bodies touch once more. Naked flesh upon naked flesh. 'You mind?'

'Do I mind you suggesting that fucking me is like fucking yourself?'

I hesitate. Then say, carefully, 'Do you think that's what it means?'

You roll over onto your front, still not looking at me, your eyes closed, as if you're trying to sleep. 'Isn't it? And…well, I suppose it makes a sort of sense.'

Part of me regrets sharing all this with you, but my interest has been piqued. 'Does it?'

'We both have blonde hair. We both – if you excuse me

flattering myself – are rather classically handsome. We seem to be able to keep ourselves in good shape without constant strenuous exercise. We're both interested in literature and art. We both would rather challenge our own sense of morality than turn and flee. So yes, it does make sense. In me, you found your literal other half, both inside and out.'

I get up suddenly, jarringly, and I feel it makes you jump. Slightly dizzy, I stumble in the darkness over to the window and look out on the grey afternoon, the mist still lingering across the grounds. After a while, I say quietly: 'I am not like you.'

Out of the corner of my eye, I see you pull yourself up on your elbows, surveying me. 'Don't get cross just because I agreed with you.' You continue to stare at me, then you say, 'I wonder if you're upset because the truth scares you. That when you look at me, you see your true self.'

I wish to God I'd never opened my mouth, that we'd just lain their together, listening to each other's breathing, satisfied and spent.

'You said that Argento levelled certain threats against you. Other than his suggestion about using Douglas's DNA.'

I nod, slowly. 'He did.'

'Tell me about them.'

I choose my words carefully, explaining to him that one of the videos Argento had shown me contained another member of my family in a 'compromising situation'.

Alastair seems almost amused by my phrasing. 'You don't have to be so coy.'

'Fine,' I say, feeling rattled now. 'It was my father. My father helping another man. The other man had killed someone

– a young woman. The footage showed my father helping him remove the body from a bedroom.'

Alastair raises his eyes. 'What happened to the tape after he showed you?'

'He kept it until the night you…that night…when I thought I'd…then he gave it to me. Of course, he could easily have kept copies, but I think he liked the ceremony of that. It was like my reward or something.'

'And you still have it now?'

'No.' I shook my head. 'I dropped it into the water, on the journey back on the boat.'

Alastair is silent for a moment then says, 'That side of things was quite convenient for you, then.'

'What do you mean by that?' I ask.

'It gave you a story you could tell yourself. When you felt bad about what happened. You could explain it away, tell yourself you had no choice. Not dig too deep into the truth.'

I'm starting to feel uncomfortable about where this is going. 'What truth?'

'That you enjoyed it more than you ever dared let on.'

I don't reply.

'Come on,' you say, suddenly brisk, 'I need you to get your clothes on. Now. There's somewhere we need to go.'

'What?' I turn round properly from the window, facing you fully. 'I'm not leaving the hotel.'

'I wasn't proposing leaving the hotel,' you say. 'Just get dressed. We're going to my bedroom.'

'I don't understand. Is my cheap, non-en-suite room here an offence to your sensibilities?'

I see you raise your eyebrows. 'Yes, I was wondering about that. Your choice of room, that is.'

'Money isn't what it used to be,' I said. 'My mother refuses to sell our family home. To say the upkeep and bills are considerable would be understating it.'

You nod. 'I understand. Well, my room is indeed much larger than this, but that isn't why I want us to go there. There's something I want to discuss. Something I want you to see. Trust me.'

'You're asking *me* to trust you?'

'Why wouldn't you?' you ask.

Images flash in front of my eyes for a split second. Images I never thought I'd have to see again. Images from a grainy video, taken twenty years ago. Images of him. And Nita. I open my mouth. Then decide it's best not to go into it. If there's one thing life has taught me, it is not to play one's cards too soon.

I let out a sigh, trying to sound more irritable than tense. 'Can't we discuss it here, whatever it is?'

'No. There are things…things I have in my room. And trust me, after what you've just told me, I think you'll be especially interested in what I have to show you.'

I shrug. 'Fine.'

For all my attempts to be dismissive and causal, I know you're not fooled. My heart is pounding, beating out a rhythm that feels unnatural, dangerous even, as if my body is warning me there is danger ahead, that this strange relationship is not a romantic meeting of minds, but something darker. A twisted connection of pitch-black souls. But still I get dressed. I still do as I'm told. I'm still unable to avoid the temptation. Temptation of finding out what you have to show me.

Once I'm fully dressed, you get up off the bed and come over and kiss me. I accept the kiss, putting my arms around you, hating both you and myself as I do so, enjoying the contrast of me being fully clothed and you without a stitch on.

You dress efficiently but without hurrying, then you walk out of the room and head to one of the upper floors via a lift near the foyer.

Your room is certainly very different to mine. It doesn't just have an en-suite, it has a bathroom bigger than my entire bedroom, and a small living room area and a bedroom with a balcony. A number of bad decisions over the years (by both myself and my family) has led to me being not exactly destitute, but unable to afford luxuries on this level.

'Sit down by the desk,' you instruct, nodding at it in the corner. I walk over, faced with the choice of an armchair or a hard-looking desk chair. I choose the desk chair, feeling like I am opting to remain alert and immune to being seduced into relaxing by the comfort of the room.

You don't sit straight away – you walk over to a cupboard and, upon opening it, start to type a code into a safe. The door of the safe buzzes and then opens and you reach inside. You take out a bag – a messenger bag, black with a silver clasp on the front. You bring it over and place it on the armchair, and from within you bring out a folder and lay it on the desk.

'Look inside,' you command.

Chapter Thirty-One

NOW

I open the folder. At first, I'm not sure what I'm looking at. It seems to be a form – like an application form, or something an employer would use, with a photograph and details like date of birth, history of residence and the like. I look up at you, and then back at the man in the picture. It looks like one of those headshots you get on corporate websites. A smiling, brown-haired man, in his later forties or early fifties. He's vaguely familiar. And then I see his name.

John Foal-Amos.

Born on the Isle of Man on 12 February.

Current residence: Shawfield Street, London, SW3.

Even after all these years, I'd never forget that name.

'How…' I look up at you, searching your face, hoping for an explanation. He watches me trying to work out what's going on here, then says: 'Argento showed me. He showed me that tape, on the night I visited his villa without you. He explained that he had told you what would happen if you didn't keep returning. I think he hoped it would help me persuade you to come back. In the end, I didn't have to remind you. But I was interested you chose to keep that little detail from me. Allowed me to think you went back for the same reason I did.'

'Which was what?' I say, frowning.

'The excitement.' You say it so casually, so easily.

I bite my lip. Look back down at the face on the page. He was handsome in his own way, with angular features, but there's a cruel slant to his smile that I can't help noticing.

'He's a guest here,' you say. 'You've probably had breakfast just metres from him.'

I look up again, now even more surprised. 'He's here? Right now?'

You nod. 'He's a very interesting character. When he's not trying to get his alcohol and drug use under control at wellness resorts, Mr Foal-Amos works for an investment bank in Aldgate. He's quite well respected there. He has substantial means and could afford to retire tomorrow, which suggests he remains in banking because he loves making money. Can't stop. And it was this need to make money that led him to the Middle East. It's perhaps unsurprising that he began to network there when he was young, cultivating important connections with everyone from fellow bankers and investors to celebrities and royalty. While he was in Qatar, in his early twenties, he attended a late-night party – although orgy would probably be a better description – in his friend's hotel suite. His friend and colleague, and another young man, brought four prostitutes back to that room for the night. In the morning, one of these women was dead. She had allegedly fallen from the balcony whilst illegally consuming alcohol.'

You reach into the bag and produce a large iPad. You place it on the desk in front of the sheet of paper, go to your camera roll and select an image. I don't recoil at the horrible picture that appears in front of me. I just stare. It is of a young woman – that much can just about be made out. Part of her face. Her open eyes. The rest of her was a mass of blood and broken limbs. Hair. Teeth.

'Was your father ever in Qatar on business in the mid-1990s?' you ask. You don't sound accusatory. You don't need to.

'I don't think we need to bring my father into this,' I say, feeling a little chill run down my back. 'He's dead now, anyway. Heart attack, ten years ago.'

'I'm sorry to hear it,' you say, although you don't sound sorry. It's as if the detail is unimportant, just a side note. 'Back to Qatar. Some arrests were made of the young men on the grounds of alcohol consumption but no charges were ever brought about over the death of the young woman. It was impossible to tell if it was an accident, a drunken fall, or something else.' You pause for a bit while we both stare at the photograph. 'Mr Foal-Amos returned to the UK with no issues at all. But he did not stay here long. He continued to travel far and wide and seemed to have business dealings of one sort or another in New Mexico, Switzerland, Sydney and…Syria. As civil war began to sweep through the country, he began to spend a lot of time at the home of a Mr Kent Al Numan. Kent isn't his original first name; he adopted it shortly before beginning his studies at Oxford University. This is how Mr Foal-Amos came to know him; they met when studying Politics, Philosophy and Economics at the same college. He remained in contact when Mr Al Numan and regularly visited him in Syria, even when safe passage became difficult because of the escalating conflicts. Mr Al Numan's home was something of a fortress in itself, away from prying eyes.'

You reach into the file, take out another photo and place it down on the desk. It shows another dead young woman. She is on a bed with what seems to be a scarf around her neck, a look of shock on her face. 'This occurred at one of the parties at Mr Al Numan's house.'

Again, I look for a feeling of revulsion within myself. I struggle to find it, even gazing into the young woman's open, staring eyes.

'She was taken to Mr Foal-Amos's bedroom during the party. She never left. Or rather, never left alive. And here is another.' You swipe across on the iPad to show a third picture. This photograph isn't of a dead body, but of a living, smiling, happy-looking young woman, in her twenties, posing for a photograph on a beach towel. 'Unlike the other two young women, this girl was British and a much riskier conquest for Mr Foal-Amos. He was attending a business conference at a hotel near Torrenova in Majorca. At the hotel was this young woman celebrating her recent graduation. This was taken the day she died. She fell from a balcony shortly before midnight that night. Apparently, she was drunk and they found ecstasy in her system, though her parents claimed she didn't take illegal drugs. The local investigation ruled it an accidental death, even though her friends claimed she had brought a man back to her hotel room that night. An older man. A man staying at the same hotel. However, there was little or no attempt made to find this man.'

I look up at you. 'I understand. This man likes killing young women. I suppose that means you have something in common.'

My words cause a flicker of something in your eyes. I think, for a moment, you're going to lash out, do something violent. But the rest of you stays completely still. 'These aren't his only crimes.'

You move over to my left-hand side to sit on the armchair. I turn to look at him.

'Mr Foal-Amos's friendship and business dealings with Kent Al Numan didn't stop at wild parties involving dead prostitutes. Al Numan was keen to start up some companies in the UK. Goods, importation, distribution. Though a number of these, upon closer scrutiny, seemed to be offshoots and subsidiaries based in various locations. Mr Foal-Amos, ever the faithful friend, provided capital and expertise in the setting up of these. He made it possible for the workers of these companies – the workers who actually existed – to afford vans and cars and other...err...equipment. You see, Mr Al Numan was keen to help fund a number of UK-based...projects, shall we say. And John Foal-Amos was more than happy to oblige. Do you see what I'm getting at, Oliver? Do you know what this man has done?'

I stare back at you, unsure where you are going with this.

'Go to the next image,' you say, quietly.

With a prickling feeling of trepidation, I turn back to the iPad and swipe. Part of me is expecting the image of another dead body or perhaps a smiling young woman – a life cut short in its prime. But instead, the screen is filled with something different. The front doors of a building. Smashed, broken glass doors, the frames barely intact. Blackened ceiling. Ambulances and police standing nearby. The sign above the doors, just about visible in its cracked, burnt state, says *Welcome to Westfield Stratford City*.

'Oh my God,' I mutter as I swipe to the left again. Another image featuring emergency services personnel. A paramedic supporting a young man, wrapping a silver blanket around him, blood running down his face. This one was taken just outside Stratford train station. There are several similar figures, wounded civilians, police officers, in the background of the photograph.

'I trust you remember the terrorist attack that happened at Stratford station and shopping centre a few years ago?'

'Of course,' I say, my voice barely a whisper.

'So now you know what type of person we're dealing with here.'

I nod.

'A person who trades in weapons, or helps line the pockets of ISIS and sponsors atrocities like this in order to protect his business relations and connections in the Middle East. The question I put to you, Oliver is a simple one. Do you think a man like this deserves to live?'

I sit back in the chair. I think about what you've just said. What you want me to say. I glance at him. Then I look back at the images on the screen in front of me. I take my time. I go back to the images of the dead women. I let my mind float back to other images of a woman's body, images I'd tried my best not to remember. Images of a woman you and I met on a Greek island one summer many years ago. I then look back at the images of carnage and terror in London. I remembered hearing about the Stratford attacks on the news. I was in the garden, digging up a fox skeleton. I don't know how it had got half-buried – whether a creature had done it or it had somehow been partially covered by dirt. I was looking at the teeth, I remember that, when I heard a shriek from the house. It was my mother. I'd gone home on her instruction to sort out the fox. She'd found it herself during one of her twilight walks in the garden; she tried to do one every day, no matter what the weather. Why the gardeners couldn't have disposed of the bones, I don't know. When I got inside, she was muttering about something, clearly upset. *I'm sorting out the skeleton*, I told her. *It will be gone soon.* But she was just pointing at the television screen. Pointing and muttering, 'I knew it, I knew it.'

The news was unfolding. The news of what had happened. For a moment, I had worried she'd heard some news, that either Douglas or Dad had been in Stratford that day for some reason. Then I heard her say, *It's exactly what the horoscopes said.* I'd become frustrated at that point. I think I said *Oh for fuck sake* or something like that, which made her angry. I told her I was going back to the garden, but she flung her arms around me and said, *Stay, stay just for a moment, we need to confront this together.* I was going to ask her what we were going confront, although I predicted it would be something to do with either my or her star signs or something. Then her hand had gone down my back to my left arm, which was still at my side. I think she'd gone to clutch at my hand, but she jumped back and screamed. It made me jump too. She pointed at my left hand. I looked down. It was covered in earth and bits of grass. And clutched in it was a bone. A jaw, to be exact. The jawbone of the little fox skeleton. The memories it conjured. I had to run outside. I only made it to the flower beds, just outside the back door, before I was sick. I crouched down on the damp grass, clutching my head, the pain not going away, hoping my mother hadn't followed me. I stayed out there for hours. She stayed in the house. It was dark before I went back in and the television was off.

As this memory comes to mind, sitting here in this comfortable, warmly lit hotel room, I look up at you and you ask me what I'm thinking about. So I tell you. All about my mother, about the television, the news report about Stratford. The fox.

'Why were you sick?' you ask.

'I think you know.' I say, quietly.

'I don't think this is helpful,' you reply. 'I think you're complicating something that's quite simple.'

'It might be simple for you,' I say, feeling something on my cheek. I touch it and am surprised to find it's a tear. And then there's another, and suddenly I'm crying, but without sobs, without gasping breaths. It's like something's finding its way out of me. Some limit in my mind has been passed and a reaction has begun to show externally – and this is the only way I can show it without screaming. Without turning violent. Even so, I feel my hands clench. And my knuckles click.

'You've felt it too, haven't you,' you say, almost whispering now. You lean in close. Your hands settle on my knee.

'Felt what?'

'The need to do it again.'

We sit with these words in silence for almost a full minute. Then you say 'I want you to help me kill this man tonight.'

I just stare at you. I don't make a sound. Just watch your

cool, steady gaze – eyes that are both intense and calm at the same time. Shining into me.

'He's staying three doors down. At the end of the corridor.'

I look at the image I've left on the iPad screen. The image of a young woman with glass in her face, blood in her hair, being helped towards an ambulance by a paramedic. I look back into your eyes.

'You're tempted, aren't you?'

I frown. I don't like being second guessed. But I can't deny to myself that you're right.

You reach forward and turn off the iPad. 'Let's take a break. You go back to your room. Wrestle with your conscience. Do what you need to do. Then, when the need to come back becomes so overpowering you can no longer ignore it, I'll be here. Shall we say midnight?'

I wait a little longer. Keeping my breathing steady. Listening to my heart quicken, then slow. I get up from the chair and walk across the room to the door. I leave without saying a word, without even looking at you, letting the door shut behind me.

Chapter Thirty-Two

NOW

I close the curtains as soon as I get into my room so I'm in complete darkness. I lie down on my bed, fully clothed, my boots still on, staring at the ceiling.

Do I want to continue down this dark rabbit hole? Am I strong enough to see where this might lead?

Slowly I allow my mind to travel back. Back to Greece. Back to our time together. There were times, as the memories struck me, I felt your hand on me. Guiding me. Pulling me towards you.

Enough, I tell myself. I force myself to rise and decide to go outside, bundling myself up in both zipped fleece and winter coat.

On the veranda, I find a group gathered around a table, each person in a winter coat similar to my own and holding a glowing orange orb in their laps. It takes me a moment to realise that they're holding jar candles, and that a man in the centre of the group is apparently telling a story, a book held up to a small candle on the little table next to him.

'…after such a journey as no mortal upon earth has ever yet taken and lived to tell the tale. I have seen the beauty and I have seen the horror of the heights – and greater beauty or greater horror than that is not within the ken of man.'

He pauses at the end of the sentence and looks up at me. 'Hello,' he says, 'Would you like to join us? We're having a little evening of spooky stories by candlelight. Although only join if you feel able to do so and it would be a safe choice.'

Safe choice? I'm puzzled by his words, and worried for a second that he is hinting at something. 'Why, what's he said?' I reply, sounding strange and irrational. Then it clicks that there are probably people suffering from addictions or mental health conditions who might find such an invitation disturbing.

'I just…sorry, who said what?' The man is frowning at me, clearly concerned. I become aware that the other five or six are all staring, turning round in their chairs. My eyes meet one of them, a woman, and as this happens she stands up and comes over to me.

'Oh it's you,' I say, probably sounding rude, but I'm not in the right frame of mind to be polite.

'Do you want to sit down?' she asks.

'No…' I say, backing away, 'No, I don't want…I can't…' I look at my watch. I have three hours until I need to be back at your room. If I decide to go back to your room.

She reaches out to me and lays a hand on my arm. 'Come on. Let's go for a walk.'

I don't argue. I'm not sure I even have the energy to.

'There's a nice path with lights on amidst the trees,' she says, 'sort of festoon-lights.' I know what she's referring to –

I'd found the little path during one of my walks around the grounds, but hadn't seen it at night all lit up. As I turn the corner and see the gravel track through the trees illuminated with seemingly floating warm-white orbs, I'm struck by how wondrous it looks – like I've been transported back to when I was a child. My mother had taken me to the local church – she was helping organise a charity concert, although from the way the vicar and his verger looked at her, I suspected she was more of a hindrance than a help. The church had been decked out with fairy lights and I'd sit on a chair at the side whilst the adults had their meeting, ignoring the book I'd brought to keep me occupied, transfixed by the lights glowing in the dark, cavernous space.

'Are you OK?' the woman asks. For a second I had forgotten I'd been brought there by this irritating stranger.

'You should go back to your group, I…' I'm not sure how to finish the sentence. I was about to say I was fine, but we both know I'm not.

'I'm not going back to the group. Come on, let's walk.' She starts up the pathway, then turns to beckon me to come.

'You're very trusting,' I say, staring around me. The whole place is deserted.

'I'm paying you the compliment of presuming you're not a murderer or psychopath or something.'

I say nothing in response. But I do follow. We walk in silence up the gravel path. Eventually, she says, 'The lights remind me of Christmas. Or weddings.'

I make a noise to show I agree.

'Are you married?' she asks.

'No. Are you?'

'I was.' She leaves it at that, so I don't press any further. I glance at her and see that her previously open, content-looking face has changed to something tighter, pinched, as if she's trying not to cry. She raises her eyes to the lights and says, 'It will be Christmas soon. They put their Christmas lights up early where I live. Many of my neighbours have country homes or villas they disappear off to in December, so they decorate in November.'

'Where do you live?'

'Kent. Well, I'm in the process of selling the house. I've decided to move to New Zealand.'

'Goodness, that's...quite a move.' Although I'd set off on this walk frustrated to be saddled with company, I was quickly realising it was what I needed. A break from the buzz and rustle of my own thoughts. Someone else to focus on.

'I know,' she says. 'I just want to get away from England. Everything. All the memories.'

We come to a stop at the top of the path, having turned uphill slightly, and are at a fork, one path leading deeper into the woods, the other to a clear shortcut back up to the west wing of the hotel.

'Which way now?' she asks, looking at me.

'I was following you.'

'Well...you must have a preference?' she says.

I don't know why, but this sudden need for a decision unsettles me, reminding me of the horrible decision that still remained weighing on me.

'What's wrong?' she asks, staring at me. I realise my distress must have shown in my face. She reaches back, her hand upon me once more, and then she comes closer and, before I have a chance to stop what is happening, her lips are on mine and she is drawing me into a kiss. I don't kiss back, but I don't leap away. Just stand there, frozen. She stops and says, 'I'm so sorry...I don't know what...I just...'

'It's fine,' I say, rubbing my face as if I've been punched. 'It's not you.'

I'm alarmed to see she's crying – not hysterically but silent tears – and she begins to dab at her eyes. 'I'm so sorry,' she says again, 'I'm just rather lonely. I came here as a bit of a break before I moved – just to, I don't know, hit reset.'

'I can understand the need to hit reset.'

'I'm so sorry,' she says again, 'You were already upset, and now I've probably made things worse. I hope this doesn't cause...any problems for you.'

I frown. 'I'm not about to start abusing prescription drugs again, if that's what you mean.'

She wipes her eyes more forcefully, then pulls her coat about her. The mist is starting to grow around us and I wonder if I should suggest we abandon our walk and return to the warmth of the hotel. Then she says something that sucks all the oxygen out of the air around us.

'I lost a child. He died in a car accident. The same time as my husband. Danny. My boy's name was Danny.'

I wait in case she wants to say more, but she just looks at the ground, so I say, 'I'm so sorry.' Then wish I had something more original, something wiser, more profound to offer her.

'It's fine. Well, of course, it isn't fine. I shouldn't be putting all this on you when it was you that was upset.'

'I'm…I'm not upset. Well, I was. I've just…It's like you said about memories. The past. I feel at a…at a crossroads.'

'You and me both,' she says, giving me a small smile. 'What's your…I mean, if you don't mind me asking, what are the options on your crossroads? What are you choosing between?'

I take a deep breath. Exhale. Watch it hit the cold air. 'I…I need to choose whether to go back to someone or not. Someone I thought I'd long since said goodbye to.'

'An ex?' she asks.

'Sort of. Someone who has just arrived back into my life.'

'And do you want her back in your life?'

'Him,' I say, 'and the truthful answer to that is that I'm not sure.'

'I'm sorry. And I shouldn't have presumed it was a woman. I should have said, "Her or him."'

'Of all the things I have on my mind today, that really isn't something I'm about to get het up about.'

'But it was wrong of me. I know that gay people don't like that – when people enforce, like, heteronormativity upon them.'

'Well, I hate to state the obvious, but "gay people" aren't one homogenous mass who all think the same thing. Maybe you shouldn't believe everything you read on Twitter. Although at least you said "gay people" and not a bundle of letters.'

She looks blank, and for a moment I worry I've been too harsh in my unsettled state, but then she simply says, 'Fair point,' and laughs, taking me by surprise. 'Although you could have been bisexual, so I suppose "gay people" might have been too limiting.'

'I'm not. But I suppose that's true.'

'Oh God, this has become all a bit awkward,' she says, shaking her head. 'I'm sorry.'

'Please stop apologising, it makes me feel like we're going round in circles.'

'We are, but that's my fault. I'm the one who kidnapped you and led you out into the forest.'

'I think it's more woodland than forest,' I say, gesturing round us.

'Another fair point. Here's a deal. I won't make this whole thing any more awkward, and in return you can walk back with me to the hotel and by the time we get there, you'll have made that decision that's troubling you. And give yourself permission to stick with it.'

I watch her for a few seconds. I can't make up my mind if any of this has been helpful, or if I'd have preferred to lie on my bed and torment myself for the rest of the evening. 'Fine, deal,' I reply. Then we start to walk back up to the hotel.

When we reach one of the side entrances, locked with a key pass, I ask if she's coming inside. 'I'm going to go back to the others. I fancy another hot chocolate, if they've not drunk them all. Are you sure I can't tempt you to join?'

'I'm sure,' I say, smiling.

'I'm sorry, I don't know your name?'

'Oliver,' I tell her. 'And yours?'

'Stephanie.' She smiles. 'I'm leaving tomorrow,' she says, 'Though I hope to meet you again.'

'It seems a bit unlikely,' I say. 'But kind of you to say.'

'Oh, you don't know. We might bump into each other. When I was younger, my mother liked to think everyone was destined to connect with most people on the planet in one way or another, even if it was just by passing them in Tesco, or by having mutual friends and acquaintances. That sort of thing.'

'Well, I'll look out for you in Tesco,' I say. I want to leave, and she seems to realise it's time. As I turn to go, she calls after me. 'What you said, about having to decide whether to go back to someone – just…don't feel pressured. I know all about wanting to relive the past. But I think it's also important we don't lose sight of the present. Make sure you're not going backwards, OK?'

I frown, trying to piece her words together. 'I'll keep that in mind. Thank you for…for the walk.' I give her a short nod, then turn to go inside.

I barely notice my journey back to my room. It's almost as if I've braced myself for the emotional upheaval of having to decide what to do.

But no such upheaval arrives. It seems I've already worked my way through it. Or perhaps I just knew all along what I would do.

The hours pass easily. I have dinner, calmly and quietly, in the more expensive balcony restaurant on one of the upper floors, overlooking the grounds. From my table I can see the twinkle of lights amidst the trees stretching out below me where I had walked earlier. My thoughts have become so extraordinarily clear. As the mist grows thicker still and starts to cover the tops of the trees and presses against the windows, my mind becomes calm, ordered, precise.

At 11.58 I start my journey. The short journey to the top of the building. The journey to you.

At midnight exactly, I knock on your door.

You open it instantly, as if you knew I'd be there.

'I knew you would come.'

Chapter Thirty-Three

NOW

Y ou invite me to sit down, this time on the comfortable chair.

'How are we going to kill him without anyone knowing?' I ask, keen to get the practical side of things sorted before we start. 'We're not on a secluded island now. And...well, I can't imagine it will be as simple.' I was going to say *and we don't have Argento to help us*, but decide this might raise more questions than I can handle at this moment.

'It will be just as simple,' you say. You walk over to a black rucksack leaning up against the desk and turn your back to me, spending a while rummaging inside. Then you come back and hold something up to the light from the desk lamp. It's a vial of clear liquid.

'You can buy anything you want on the dark web.'

'What's inside it?'

'You don't want to know.'

'But what if I do?'

You take in a breath, then says, 'It's retribution. And absolution. All in one tiny bottle.'

'I don't want to offer him absolution.'

You raise your eyebrows at me. 'Now that I can understand.' You slowly reach out and take my hand. I let you. You run your fingers across my palm. Move in close. Your hand putting the small vial of clear liquid in mine. 'If you don't think he deserves absolution, you should be the one to offer the retribution.' You say this in almost a whisper, your mouth close to my ear. I nod. With your other hand you touch my cheek, then step back. 'We should leave in just under two hours,' you say.

I'm confused by this. 'Then why did you ask me to come here at midnight?'

You raise your eyebrows once again, but this time the movement isn't questioning. It's suggestive. 'Why do you think?' you say, starting to unbutton your shirt.

I lie in your bed, your right arm slung over me. I can hear your heavy breathing and I wonder if you're asleep. I slowly ease myself out of the bed and check the time. It's one-thirty in the morning. Not long to go now. I pad quietly along the soft carpet over to the balcony, pulling back the curtains, opening the doors. I look back at you, lying quietly on your side, your face turned into the pillow. For a second, the years pull me back once more. Then the cold night air hits my skin and reminds me where I am. How much time has passed. Not just summer into winter, but years into decades. Youth into adulthood. But I'm still the same inside. I know that now.

I step out onto the small balcony, enjoying the sensation of the cold hard floor under my toes, the misty chill enveloping me. I look down into the night, just making out the grass of the lawn and the shape of trees through the mist. And down there, in shimmering darkness, I think I see her. Stephanie. Watching me, in the middle of the lawn, swirls of the fog wrapping around her. I give a sharp intake of breath and step backwards, clutching the side of the balcony door to steady myself. When I look back, there's nobody there. No one at all.

'Are you all right?' you ask.

'Fine,' I reply, although it's a lie. I walk to the bed and begin to pull on my clothes. 'We should go now.'

'Keen?' you ask, looking amused.

'Ready,' I reply, staring straight at him.

Chapter Thirty-Four

NOW

W e walk along the corridor. Part of me had expected it to be dark, perhaps swirling with mist like the grounds outside. But it is as brightly lit as it had been when I'd walked along it a couple of hours previously.

'Won't there be CCTV?' I whisper as we leave the room.

'That will be sorted,' you say, simply. Perhaps I am foolish to have such confidence in you, but you always manage to appeal to that part of me that wants to throw caution to the wind. Abandon all sense of logic, reason, any notion of right or wrong. So I go with you, obediently as ever.

We walk to a room three doors down from the one we left. I watch as you take out a key card and insert it into the slot. The door opens a slight crack as you push it gently with your hand. And I can see that there's a light on inside.

'Wait,' I whisper, suddenly thinking of all the things I should have checked with you before we got to this moment. 'What if he's not asleep?'

'He'll be asleep,' you whisper back. The certainty in your voice is what I need to hear.

We walk in. As soon as I'm in the room, I feel a wave of relief when I see a man's form passed out on the bed. Mr Foal-Amos is asleep on top of the covers. He's lying on his front, wearing blue-checked pyjama bottoms. His face is only partly visible, his fringe flopping down over his forehead, his head half off the pillow. From the outline of his arms I see his muscles. It's like strength radiates off him. Then my mind flicks to the bodies of the young women. The women he must have overpowered. The women he must have frightened, hurt, abused before their deaths. Women who would have entered hotel rooms like this.

'I made sure there was something extra in his after-dinner coffee,' you whisper. 'He won't wake up.'

'Then why didn't you just…' I start to whisper back, then stop myself.

You turn and walk back towards me, slowly, looking me in the eye. 'Why didn't I just kill him then?' You raise an eyebrow, then let a hand snake round my waist, pulling me into a kiss. 'Where would be the fun in that?' you say, letting your hand start roving downwards. I stop him before he gets anywhere.

'Not here,' I say, looking over at the bed.

'He honestly won't wake. We can even talk in normal voices,' you say, raising your volume, 'although it would be prudent to keep our tone slightly low, perhaps. Just in case.' You nod to the door we've just come in by and I realise you mean the corridor outside. I nod and break away from you.

'Let's just get it over with,' I say.

'That's not the spirit to enter this with,' you reply, now looking slightly disappointed.

'It's the way I like to work,' I say. 'I find it best not to linger.'

'Strange,' you say, still looking at me, 'Maybe we're not so alike after all.'

For a moment I think you're about to say something else, then you pull up the shoulder bag and open the top. You pull out two clear plastic bags that appear to hold a number of objects. You put your shoulder bag down, unzip one of the plastic bags, and take out what looks like one of the mugs from the downstairs restaurant. You then place it by the side of the bed.

'What are you doing?' I ask, even though I have a general idea.

'Confusing the crime scene,' you reply. You then take out a scrunched-up tissue and drop it by the side of the bed. Now for the other bag, which holds a pair of black sports socks. You lay the sports socks over the radiator on the far side of the room. 'Women's underwear would have been more ideal,' you say, 'but I have to work with what I could get hold of.'

'Where have you got all those things from?' I ask.

'The hotel. Collected them. Used by different guests. It's amazing what you can pick up, here and there, if you keep your eyes open, people can be so untidy with their belongings. They may not all be tested, it depends how rigorously the room is processed by forensics, but there's enough there for them to puzzle about for a good long while, I think.'

I go over to your shoulder bag and reach inside. There's

another clear plastic bag containing a toothbrush and comb. 'I'm presuming these aren't yours?' I ask.

'You presume right,' you say, reaching out for the bag and taking it from me. 'I'm going to put them in the bathroom. Again, it will just make things a little less clear.'

You do as you say while I take out something else from the bag. The small snakeskin wallet.

When you come out of the bathroom, I turn round to see that you've removed your jumper and top and are in the process of unbuckling your trousers.

'What are you…?'

'Come on, Oliver,' you say, coming over to me, whispering in my ear once more. 'Let's do it here, on the floor while we watch him die.'

I no longer feel the rush of shivers run down my spine as your face brushes against my neck. I'm tired of your games.

'I'm ready to do what we came to do,' I say, giving you a slight push so that you move out of my way. I walk over to the bed and set what I'm holding down on the covers next to the man. Unzip the case and take out the syringe and clear vial.

'Get out the way,' I say, moving round to the end of the bed and pushing you aside. 'Put your clothes back on. We're leaving as soon as I've done this.'

'Yes, sir,' you say, a little sarcastically, but in a way that shows you're liking my assertiveness. I pull up the material a little on the left leg of Mr Foal-Amos's pyjama trousers to fully expose his ankle. I can hear you buckling up your belt and tugging on your jumper as I lean over close and push the syringe into the chosen patch of flesh. Then I straighten up.

'We're leaving,' I say. 'Now.'

I don't look back at you. Nor do I glance at the man on the bed. I need to get out of the room and away from what's happened here. And I'm sure that you'll follow me.

I'm right. You walk to the doorway and lay your hands on my shoulders. Before we step back out to the corridor, you whisper to me earnestly, 'How do you feel now?'

I allow my eyes to fix on you. Feel my heart beating fast, adrenaline rushing through me. 'Alive,' I reply. 'I feel alive.'

Chapter Thirty-Five

NOW

A fter leaving Mr Foal-Amos's room, I presume we'll return to your suite. But instead, you stop me as I head to your door.

'This way,' you say, nodding to the stairs.

So I follow you. Follow you down to the swimming pool and spa. Pass the empty reception area and the opening times saying the area closed at 10.30pm. Nothing is locked, though, and you press on until we are at the poolside where we'd sat just hours earlier. It feels like days, weeks, months even have gone by since we lay on the reclining seats. Time itself has taken on a new form and I am getting lost within it, both the present and the past.

'Let's go for a swim,' you say to me.

I look around us and note a security camera in the corner.

'I told you to stop worrying about that,' you say when you see what I'm looking at. You set your bag down by one of the loungers and begin to strip. You don't even bother to keep your briefs on this time, just pull everything off and walk naked down the steps into the pool.

'Come on,' you say to me. 'For old times' sake.'

'I think we've done enough for old times' sake,' I say, but part of me is tempted. Tempted to feel the water lapping against my skin. Washing away everything that's happened today. Birthing me anew.

'Please,' you say, your eyes seeking out mine.

I look at you, then smile and nod. I go over to the lounger where you left your clothes and pull off mine, leaving them scattered next to the bag. Then I follow you into the pool. You've been floating on your back, near the far side, but swim over to me as I enter the water, sending waves lapping against my legs as the steps take me deeper. As soon as I'm submerged, you pull me into your arms and into a passionate kiss.

'This is how it was always meant to be,' you whisper to me, moving your mouth to my ear, breathless and excited. I felt you hardening against me and I put my hand out to take hold of you, hear your groan of desire. 'We were meant to be in this life together. We were meant to tread this path as two, not one. And we can carry on. This is only the start.'

You spin me around so that my hands are gripping the sides of the pool, your face kissing down my neck to my shoulders, your arms going round me. I pull back my hand, lay it on yours to stop you. 'No,' I said, 'I…I won't do it without a condom.'

'Oh come on,' you say, clearly desperate for the moment not to pause.

'I'll get it,' I say, pulling myself out the pool.

'There's one in the right-hand pocket of my jeans,' you say, nodding to the pile of clothes. I go over and take out the condom from your trousers. Then, I open the bag.

When I turn back, I expect you to be watching me, but thankfully you've returned to floating on your back, staring up at the blue-turquoise lights causing the reflection of the water to dance hypnotically on the ceiling.

I sit on the side of the pool, letting my legs drop into the water. But I don't slide in completely. I want you to come to the edge. I want you to touch. Feel your hands on mine. Feel you for the final time.

You do as I'd hoped. As you touch my legs, taking hold, I start to speak. 'The question I've been pondering all evening,' I say, keeping my tone level, 'is how John Foal-Amos came to be staying in the very hotel I'm staying in. The very hotel *you're* staying in.'

I then pull my hands round to my front. By the time you see what I'm holding, it's too late. Too late for you to do anything. Too late for you to stop me. I push the needle in firmly. It's over within a second or two.

I see the shock in your eyes. The man who never likes to be surprised. Who always knows everything before it's happened, or acts as if he does. And now I've got you. Shocked you beyond anything you've seen.

You make a sound that could have been 'Ohhh' or 'Hey' or 'How'. I'm not too sure. But you pull away from me, even though it's too late. All the liquid from the vial has gone into you.

'It's *him*, isn't it,' I whisper, but I don't know if my words can be heard over the noise of the water splashing as you

continue to move back, away from me. I want you to hear, I
need you to hear, so I make myself talk louder. 'All of this has
been down to *him*,' I say, more clearly, pushing my voice into
the echoing space. 'Argento has orchestrated this. Why else
would you be here? For all your talk about us being meant to
be together, you haven't bothered to find me before now. But
I'm not playing his game. Not anymore. Not with you.

'But you've always underestimated me, haven't you?
Always presumed I'm second-rate to you, playing catch-up.'

'What…' you gasp, dragging yourself to the steps, 'Why…
what are you talking about?'

'You've always treated me as if I'm disposable. You make
me fall into your arms, make me *need* you, and then you do
something that reminds me how shallow your feelings really
are.'

'I don't know what you're—'

You've got a foot onto the lower step now and are shakily
pulling yourself round, trying to stand properly.

'You're the one who's come second place, now, Alastair.'

'What…why…why now?' you try to shout, but your ability
to talk is already fading. 'If you could have killed me back then
– truly deliberately killed me – why…why didn't you?'

I stare back at you, defiant. 'You believed what I said about
worrying I'd mixed up the coffee mugs. I *had* accidentally
mixed them up, but it was you I meant to kill, not Sir Hector. If
only I'd passed the right cup to you, we wouldn't be here now.
And you underestimated me again just now, presuming I
would do as you say, presuming I had injected Foal-Amos. You
didn't even check if the vial was still full.'

You're struggling to stand now. I wait a few seconds,

watching you find putting one foot in front of the other the most difficult task in the world. Then I go over and help you out of the pool. You're growing faint. Fading quickly. I lead you slowly over to one of the loungers and lay you down. 'They're going to think this is a suicide. And to be honest, this death is a mercy,' I say, then lower my voice to a whisper, pressing my lips close to your ear. 'Because I saw what you did to Nita, all those years ago. Argento had it on video. You didn't just inject her. All those tools he had weren't just for show, were they? You used them on her. On her skin. On her bones. On her neck, on her jaw. You indulged in her death, the same way you indulged in fucking her and indulged in deceiving me. So when all is considered, I think you're getting it pretty easy, don't you?'

You laugh quietly, almost as if to yourself. Slowly, your eyes return to my face, although it's clear you're now struggling to focus. 'You still have no idea, do you,' you say, a slight smile now visible. 'We never bumped into each other by chance. We never had a summer romance or whatever you've been telling yourself...why else do you think I fucked Nita? I wanted...I liked...the thrill of it all...' You're starting to become weak, your speech slurred. But you've got me. Once again, you've drawn me in with your words. And for the last time, I lean in to listen, desperately needing to know what you were going to say. When you don't speak again, I shake you, telling you to finish what you were trying to say. 'I'm his nephew...,' you say, very quietly, 'He told me to...to...bring you...You and me...none of it was ever...real.'

I say nothing. The power of speech has now left me. My emotions soaring, peaking, then, just as quickly, falling. So that by the time the tears have started to fall down my face, my eyes have become dry again. My feelings numb. Whether this is self-preservation, my mind trying to protect me from a level of personal horror I'll never be able to face, or I've truly travelled beyond the realms of normal human emotion, I don't know. But there's no good to be found in wallowing in it. I just sit, as it becomes impossible for you to talk any more.

I leave as soon as I see the life has left your eyes.

Epilogue

I wait outside the gates of the wellness centre. It's dark, the dawn still just a distant prospect, so I should see a car approaching from quite a distance away. He'll come. I know he'll come. As the architect of all this, he wouldn't want to be far away. And all it takes is one message. A text to tell him an immediate exit is needed.

I've taken myself off to a separate part of my head – a part that I think of as a mental waiting room, where I can sit still, calm within myself, just after I've experienced something. Something extreme. It's a tactic I learnt years ago during the sessions on Argento's island. It allowed me not to feel horror or repulsion about what happened there. And then, when I continued to return, year after year, every summer, for nearly ten years, it became a habit. But it's been a while since I've needed to work this hard to get myself into a state of mind fit for me to function. Even though the murder I've just committed is one I've considered myself guilty of for most of my adult life, it's hard to ignore the part of me that's rebelling against my reasoning, trying to tempt me into a state of shock, a state of dismay. You were alive – I'd been offered another chance. Another chance with you. A chance at a life lived together. A ghost, back from the dead, made real, into flesh and blood, just for me. And I'd extinguished that chance all over again.

By the time I see the flicker of lights on the road in the distance, I've got myself under control. But as soon as the Range Rover draws up outside the gates and the door opens for me to get inside, I feel things starting to disintegrate again. Something rises within me. Anger. I toss my bag onto the back seat and get in. Two men are seated in the front. Only one of them looks round.

'You lied to me all this time,' I say, feeling suddenly breathless as if I'd been running. 'He's your nephew. Your *nephew*. He kept that from me. *You* kept that from me. You let him disappear from my life, allowing me to think I'd killed him. All these years—'

'Calm down,' Argento says quietly.

'You knew he would be there. You knew we'd both be guests at the same time.'

Argento stares at me, his expression unreadable. Then, when he talks again, his voice is calm, gentle even, clearly attempting to soothe me. 'I'm sorry, Oliver. Please forgive an old man his little games.'

'Games? *Games*? We've spoken about this before. I'm not a pawn in some game for you to play with. Complete honesty between us both. That's what we agreed, when I came back to you. If I can't trust that, I don't know what's the point anymore...I...I thought you valued that.'

'And I still do,' he says. He reaches out and taps my knee, like a kindly uncle trying to placate a troublesome nephew who is close to having a tantrum. He then turns back round and speaks to the man to his right. 'When you are ready.'

The driver doesn't acknowledge me at all as he looks back to reverse the car and then steers it out onto the road.

'Don't you care?' I ask, annoyed at his evasion. 'Your nephew is dead. Don't you care at all?'

Argento seems to consider this for a moment. Then he says, 'Life is complete. Whatever its length may be.'

We carry on in silence through the countryside, the headlights only illuminating the night a few metres in front of us as we press on through the darkness. Then a question arises that I feel I need to ask before we continue. 'You're going to sort the CCTV? The pool side. There was at least one camera around there.'

'Relax, my dear Oliver,' he says, without looking round. 'It will all be taken care of.'

I allow a minute or two to pass, before I speak again. 'I presume you brought the two of us together deliberately but… well, to what end? To see who killed the other first?'

Argento looks up at me in the rear-view mirror. I can see that he is smiling. 'Whatever the outcome, it would have been an interesting experience for you both,' he says, slowly and carefully. 'And that, after all, is what we live for, isn't it, Oliver? *Experience*. Otherwise you wouldn't have stayed in contact with me all these years.'

I say nothing. Thoughts swirl and spin through my head. When I don't respond for a full five minutes, Argento orders his driver to stop the car.

'Pull over just up there,' he says.

Surprised, I watch as Argento gets out of the front passenger seat and then opens my door.

'Get out of the car.'

I stare at him, confused. Then I unbuckle my seat belt and slide out. Argento walks slightly away from the car – maybe to be out of earshot of Luke, or perhaps just to stretch his legs after a long journey. I follow, but keep back a little, unsure of what's going on.

'The world is changing, Oliver. You may feel it. I think many people do. I do not think it's an overstatement to say that our way of life is heading for a change of such magnitude, I want to set up a base for when the time comes.'

I frown at him. 'What sort of base?'

He takes a step closer to me. 'A community. We've found a section of land within a forest in Northumberland. There we will bring together a group of like-minded people who understand what it's like to live a life that can truly transcend the mundane rules and closed-minded attitudes that so many people live by. We need to surround ourselves with people *like us*.' His eyes are fixed on mine, and not for the first time I feel as if he's able to read every thought, examine every desire, view every memory within me. 'So I am giving you the choice, Oliver. Join me properly, get back in the car, and we'll build something remarkable together. Or walk away now. I promise you'll never hear from me again.'

It's like I have spent the whole journey in a vacuum until that point. And suddenly, the vacuum has been compromised and the world returns, rushing and roaring, energising every sense within me. The forest on either side of us suddenly seems alive with birds, with swaying trees. It is as if I can hear every living creature within its beating heart, every scamper of a field mouse, every swish of a tail, every beat of a wing. Every sound is pulling me towards it, as if encouraging me, calling me in. I understand what this means as easily as I understand that I am human and I am breathing. If I walk away now, I will be choosing life. Choosing freedom. If I go with Argento, continue to participate in his ideas and twisted games, no matter how grand they sound, I will be choosing death.

I take one last look at the man who has infected my life for too long, then walk away. I grab my bag from the car seat, then set off, not bothering to say goodbye, not caring that this is potentially the end to many extraordinary years. Terrible in many ways, occasionally terrifying – but yes, extraordinary.

I walk down the country road through the blackness, keeping my eyes on the sky. The clouds are starting to part, offering a welcome glow of moonlight.

Ten minutes. That's all it takes. I manage ten minutes, before I look over my shoulder.

The car is still there, its lights illuminating the ground and trees around it.

He knows. Knows I won't get far. Knows I won't really leave him. And I know it too.

Acknowledgments

Special thanks to my family: Leno, for continued kindness and encouragement throughout the writing process, my parents, sisters Molly and Amy, granny and uncle, and to Rebecca and Tom and all my close friends. Thanks to Simon Masters and Fiona Cummins for always being there for chats and support (and delightful lunches!).

I would like to thank my wonderful agent Joanna Swainson and everyone at Hardman & Swainson for being such a brilliant team. Huge thanks to my editor Jennie Rothwell and to Kimberley Young, Charlotte Ledger, Emma Petfield, Lucy Bennett, Arsalan Isa, Chloe Cummings and everyone at One More Chapter and HarperCollins. I'm overjoyed to be part of an amazing publisher family. Thanks also to my former editor Bethan Morgan for her support and early feedback on this book and for such amazing work on previous novels.

A massive thank you to all the booksellers who have been so brilliant at pressing my novels into the hands of readers and to the authors who so generously read early proofs of this book and offered such kind words.

Last but not least, I'd like to say a huge thanks to all the readers who have picked up my previous books and taken time to recommend them to friends, leave reviews online and post about them on social media. I'll always been extremely grateful.

Author Q&A

1. What was your inspiration for writing *Notes on a Murder*?

This may sound strange, but it was actually the weather outside when I wrote it! I wrote most of this book during the July 2022 heatwave as I had been inspired by the hot weather to write a summer romance novel with a dark thriller edge. As soon as I'd had that initial moment of inspiration, the plot came to me almost instantly.

2. Which was your favourite character and/or scene to write?

Although they're a bit nasty, the scenes in the dungeons/cages were creatively the most interesting to write as that whole thread of the story was a lot darker than anything I'd written recently. I think I always want to write thrillers that are a bit different, rather than feeling like I'm going back over old ground, and although that aspect to the plot does have a slight connection to my 2019 novel *A Version of the Truth*, I felt it was a new area of crime-fiction-bordering-on-horror that was interesting to explore.

3. How do you choose names for your characters?

It takes a while to find character names I haven't used before! I usually pick them from 'baby names' websites intended for prospective parents, and then make sure they fit the sort of names the characters would have for their background.

4. How do you come up with ideas for writing thrillers?

They usually arrive through watching old films or TV shows, although it's normally more of a 'vibe' about something that inspires me, rather than a plot or characters.

5. *Notes on a Murder* is your sixth book, has your writing process changed since you published your first book?

My first two novels were published when I had a full-time job, so I had a bit of a different process and routine. Since then, the amount of time I spend writing is probably about the same across a whole week, but I have a lot more time to do things like research trips and absorbing other works of art (usually novels or films) for inspiration. In terms of the writing of the novels, the thing that's been the same about my process ever since my first book has been meticulous chapter-by-chapter planning. I don't think I'd be able to write a book without doing this.

6. Are there any specific authors who have inspired your writing?

There are loads! I'd say Ruth Rendell is probably the biggest inspiration, both with her psychological thrillers and detective mysteries written under her own name and with the standalone novels written as Barbara Vine. Other authors would include Liane Moriarty, Karin Slaughter and Ian McEwan (although that's just three out of hundreds!).

7. What does a typical day in the life of B P Walter look like? Do you have to stick to a strict writing routine?

I do generally stick to a routine, although it's one I can adapt if other things have to occur (like trips away or fun outings!). But presuming there's nothing like that in the calendar, then a typical day starts with going out for a run, usually accompanied by an audiobook. Once I'm back home I'll then select my viewing material for the day – I like to have three or four things lined up, both movies and TV shows, as these will the things I'll have on the TV while I'm writing. I don't like writing in silence, and I find having the TV on is both comforting and inspiring in a creative sense. The movies and shows I watch have to be things I've seen before, otherwise they'll distract me! But providing they're films and dramas I'm familiar with, they provide the perfect writing environment for me. I use the morning to get the 'main work' of the day done, which is normally writing (unless there's anything particularly pressing in terms of social media or tax admin stuff!). I never keep track of how many words I've written – I'll just stop as soon as it gets to lunchtime and go to the gym or the swimming pool. After that, it's rare I'd carry on writing (sometimes I do, but it would be a different book to the one I'd worked on in the morning). I'd usually use the afternoon to either watch new films or TV series or go to a coffee shop to read. I see reading new fiction and watching screen content as the most important thing I do for my process – it's like going to a creative well. I then might do some social media things or email admin, before putting away my work for the day.

Read on for an extract from *The Locked Attic*

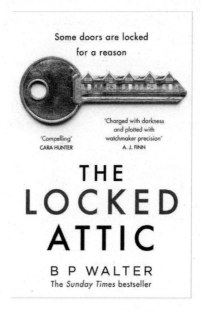

Some doors are locked
for a reason

'Compelling'
CARA HUNTER

'Charged with darkness
and plotted with
watchmaker precision'
A. J. FINN

THE
LOCKED
ATTIC

B P WALTER
The *Sunday Times* bestseller

Available to order in eBook and paperback now

The Locked Attic: Extract

Chapter 1, Stephanie, 7 months before the explosion

It's hard to really know where this all started.

When I first met my husband? When we had our boy? When we moved to Oak Tree Close? They all vaguely feel like beginnings in some way. But I think the day that properly set the wheels in motion was the late October night I picked up my sixteen-year-old son Danny from his band practice at his mate Scotty's. The band practice had actually become a sort of party to celebrate Scotty's seventeenth birthday, which was officially the following week, but Danny would be in America then and I think a few of the others couldn't make it. So the party was tacked on to the end of their normal Friday night band practice. My husband had dropped him off, and even though he said he didn't mind going back to get him, I could tell he didn't want to venture out in the cold again. So I said I'd go.

I hadn't really wanted Danny to go to the party, but Pete

said it was harsh to make the boy miss out just because we were going away the next day. 'He won't be able to sleep. He'll be excited anyway, so he might as well be hanging out with his friends.' I told him teenagers grow out of that so-excited-I-can't-sleep routine before a holiday, and besides, him being awake and out partying means *we* have to be awake – something that, at the age of sixteen, he probably hadn't quite clocked.

The temperature was falling fast and the light in the car had gone off, making the street lamps along the road seem even brighter, glowing in a thin mist that was starting to spread through the night air. I noticed the house to my left had Halloween decorations strung through the trees – warm-white fairy lights intertwined with a sequence of pumpkins and fake orange leaves. They'd probably just remove the pumpkins once the 31st had passed; that way they'd already have their Christmas lights up, prepped and ready. They put them up early around here, probably because so many of the families jetted off to their holiday homes in December. We'd never done that – a proper British Christmas was what Pete liked and, over the years, I'd grown to like it too. It had never been that much fun with my parents, but I'd got into the swing of things when I had kids of my own. Watching Danny tear open his presents really had been that special kind of magic so many parents talk about, especially when he was younger.

I was drawn out of my seasonal nostalgia by a noise from over near Scotty's house. The front door had opened and two figures had started walking along the path through the front garden and over towards me.

'Hi, boys,' I said, as Danny and Jonathan got in. I'd

completely forgotten we were giving Danny's bandmate and schoolfriend Jonathan Franklin a lift, although since he lived practically opposite us it didn't really make much of a difference. I was used to ferrying him about, and at least the Franklins often returned the favour.

'Good party?' I asked, when neither of them replied to my cheery greeting. I started driving, wondering what on earth was going on. I usually got a 'Hiya' at the very least from Danny, and Jonathan wasn't a rude, unfriendly boy, although he could be a little shy.

There was something else different too, something I realised as I manoeuvred the car out of the tight cul-de-sac and onto Elm Tree Road, which was just one of the many rabbit-warren-like streets that made up our neighbourhood. Danny was in the front with me, his guitar clutched between his legs. He didn't usually do this, not when we had Jonathan in the car. They'd always sit in the back and talk about things – trivial stuff, like the fact Scotty always played his guitar slightly flat, or something that had happened in maths class and why Mr Redmond was 'such a prick'. But nothing was said at all. Silent and separated, they just sat as I drove, an awkward tension seeming to radiate off both of them.

'Is everything OK?' I asked, and Danny finally stirred, jerking his head towards me as if he'd only just realised I was there. 'Oh fine, yeah… just tired.'

He wasn't just tired. I knew something was wrong. But it didn't look like he was going to elaborate, not while Jonathan was in the car. Nor did he seem keen to hang around when we got home, after his friend had sloped off to his own house over the road. He just disappeared upstairs, swiftly followed by his father, asking if he had everything packed for the flight tomorrow.

And that was that.

He behaved relatively normally the next day, was generally fine in America, if a tad quiet, while we stayed with Pete's brother. It was only once we returned and the days started to edge into winter that that odd night in the car with the two boys came back into my mind. And everything went spinning off in another direction. A direction that both changed my world and obliterated it.

Chapter 2, Stephanie, the day of the explosion

I was having a dream when the first explosion occurred. Something about my wedding day, but we couldn't find any flowers – someone had stolen them from the church, and then we ended up finding them in a Tesco bag-for-life out in the graveyard, swimming in blood. It was all rather horrible, especially when the vicar, who was the spitting image of Frank Sinatra, poured gasoline onto them, cackling as he did it, and created a mini blaze amongst the gravestones. Stranger still, my mother was there, looking delighted, which was a rarity in itself, and stood behind the burning flowers singing 'We Three Kings', the song she'd sung to me as a child, no matter what time of year it was. Desperate to take hold of her, I reached out my hand, stretching, trying to reach her.

But the explosion put an end to all that.

I was pulled into reality in an instant, flailing around in my duvet, looking about me, unsure where the noise was coming from. It was so loud, and deep, with a heavy bass resonance so strong it was almost as if I could still feel it vibrating within me.

I felt both alert and disorientated as I scrabbled around on the bedside table for my phone. I picked it up and looked at the time. 6.45am. I scrolled through the in-built news app, then BBC News, but couldn't find any reports. I opened up Twitter and typed in *Kent* and *Bang*. Someone called CassieLovesZayn had tweeted:

OMFG what the fuck was that? MASSIVE bang. Anyone else in Hangway in Kent hear it?

A guy simply called Gavin had replied:

Yeah, love. Massive. Definitely a bomb.

Although I wasn't any more of an expert than Gavin, I had to agree with him – a noise that loud certainly sounded like a bomb blast, or at least what I'd imagine one to sound like. But there wasn't anywhere around here someone would want to attack. We weren't near any tourist landmarks that would result in mass fatalities. I was continuing to scroll when I saw a woman named LexieStarSigns had tweeted:

The power station has gone up, it's on fire! I can see it from my house!

I rushed to the balcony. The trees were too high for me to see much, but there was something there that wasn't usually part of my morning view. A dark, ominous layer, getting larger, blossoming and growing and starting to fill the sky above the trees and the woodland my house backed onto.

I returned to my bed. Was I in danger? If the power station had gone up, was I at risk of shrapnel falling on my house or smoke inhalation or something? Whilst the thought of my own death no longer troubled me, I still didn't really like the idea of choking amidst the unfurling carpet of black smoke crawling its way across the horizon.

I spent the best part of the next half hour sitting on my bed, scrolling through social media, checking what people were saying and watching the news organisations steadily get pictures and reports up on their websites; some embedded tweets from the public amidst their reporting, including the ones I'd already read, along with a statement from Kent Police saying they were dealing with a 'major incident' and in the process of evacuating nearby residences within a two-mile radius of the power station. All other residents within the Hangway area must apparently stay inside their houses and keep away from windows.

In spite of the advice, I returned to the French windows of the bedroom and went out onto the balcony. The sky was growing darker with the smoke now and there was a strange scent in the air. Burning, yes, but something else, something nasty and chemical-smelling. I went back inside and started to wander through the dark house. Though the day wasn't especially chilly, it was cold out on the landing. Perhaps the chill came from how empty the place was. Large empty houses were sad things. All that space just felt so unnecessary. I never used the cinema room, or the home gym, or the swimming pool anymore. I kept mostly to my bedroom, interspersed with trips to the kitchen to get myself bowls of cereal or to the hallway to take in deliveries.

It was when I went down to the kitchen to make myself a coffee that I realised the power wasn't working. I glanced at my phone and saw that it had no connection to the house Wi-Fi. Instead of coffee, I had a glass of orange juice, congratulating myself for it still being fresh and drinkable. I wasn't a totally pathetic recluse, I thought to myself as I journeyed back upstairs. I didn't let food go off; I still ate reasonably well. But in spite of that, things were far from calm in my world. I was always teetering on the edge of reality and something else, something more dangerous but still strangely tempting. Madness, perhaps? I don't think I ever properly lost my grasp, not completely. There were nights when I thought I had literally gone mad with my grief and I'd never pull myself out. But then the spell would break and the dawn would come and I would be sitting there, clutching a pillow, realising I was both starving and thirsty and I would manage to pull myself up, take a shower and carry on with my day. My day inside, doing nothing much but existing. Reading books. Tidying. Watching TV without any real interest or enjoyment. It's a cruel irony that these are the things I never felt like I had the time to do when everything was how it was meant to be. I always wished I had more free time. I never expected to end up with too much of it.

Instead of going back to my room, I went to Danny's bedroom. It still showed evidence of his younger self, before he became a teenager. A large stack of boardgames remained at the bottom of his wardrobe that he hadn't touched since he was ten. Some plush cuddly toys from Disney movies like *Lilo*

& Stitch and *Monsters, Inc.* were under the bed – too embarrassing for him to have had on show, but too loved to be discarded completely. On the surface level, some things had changed though. The posters of *Harry Potter* had been taken down and replaced with ones of video games that I knew next to nothing about. I didn't like them – they featured angry-looking men and overly sexualised women and cars. They gave the room an edge I didn't like. Something a bit hard and laddish, something I didn't want my son to turn into. I went over to his bed and sat down cross-legged on it. I was tempted to curl back up into the covers and breathe in his smell and get lost in a world of memories, but I knew I shouldn't do that. If I did that, I wouldn't leave for hours. Images of his childhood would flash before me, as if projected into the darkness of my mind by a beam of light both dim and vivid, flickering and ultra-sharp. Him splashing about in his paddling pool on the balcony garden when we had our London flat. Him running through the leaves in the park, kicking them into the air, laughing and shrieking. And more recent moments that I can't escape, no matter how much I want to. His change of behaviour. His moods. The secrets he wouldn't share. And the things he knew that I so wished he hadn't.

I stared out at my dead son's belongings and couldn't help but feel the crushing weight of everything in the room pressing down on me. All the things he'd owned, all the toys he'd played with, all the clothes he'd worn, all the books he'd read and the movies he'd watched. And mingled amongst them, all the things he'd never do, all the clothes he'd never wear again, all the books he'd never get around to reading, all the movies he'd never watch. All the secrets he'd never share. And there were a fair number of those in here, I was sure of that. Things I would probably never know. Things I'd been in the middle of uncovering just before it all happened. Before everything ended.

The day my husband and son were killed.

Chapter 3, Stephanie, four months before the explosion

The last conversation with my husband before he died was a stupid spat about how he'd got the washing mixed up and seemed to have lost a number of my things and Danny's rugby shorts in the process. It wasn't the first time things had gone missing – a favourite dress of mine had vanished, one I'd wear for special occasions, like a rare evening out to a posh restaurant with Pete, along with some of my underwear and shorts. Pete had said they must be in my cupboard and I just wasn't looking properly. I took everything out and put it back again, just to prove him wrong.

'Whilst I love it when you try to be helpful, I think perhaps you should just leave the laundry to me,' I'd said bluntly as I flung my things back in, coat hangers scraping as metal hit metal.

'You're always saying I should do more myself while we find a new housekeeper,' he moaned as I rather dramatically swung the cupboard doors shut. I still had Danny's PE kit to sort out. Part of me wondered if Danny should be doing this himself, now that he was sixteen and it was his own choice to be playing football after school. I was also furious that, after what had happened the night before, this day – the penultimate day of the Christmas holidays – wasn't the calming, healing day we'd planned. Granted, Danny had seemed much better during the morning, trying to reassure us he was OK after what had happened the night before. He had given me such a fright.

The mention of a potential housekeeper led to another mini-argument, something I was trying to avoid. With something evidently on Danny's mind, I had hoped Pete and I could have avoided petty squabbles for one day at least, just whilst we tried to find out what was going on. It was stupid, the idea that we should have someone cleaning our house and washing our clothes and doing the ironing when we could easily do it ourselves. I only worked part-time at the local travel agent's in the high street, and Pete had started to take more of a backseat role in his company. It wasn't like we didn't have the time. Although time did still seem to run away with us, and, even though I hated to admit it, part of me did miss having someone doing everything for us when we'd lived in our house on Warwick Square in central London. Upon moving to Kent, I had been adamant that a luxury like that wasn't 'an essential' and although I relented and allowed Pete to employ a cleaner who came in once a week, a 'housekeeper' felt way too old-fashioned and more like something you'd find in *Downton Abbey* than in a house in the suburbs.

Pete and I had been so caught up in our disagreement, I'd forgotten the plan for the afternoon: that Danny was to go to the cinema with his dad to cheer him up, followed by a pizza together. Pete was going to get to the root of what had been wrong with him for the past few months. And what had caused the unsettling drama of the night before. But all this was thrown into disarray when Danny asked if he could go round his friend Scotty's for band practice. The request made me instantly anxious. 'But... you and the band haven't got together for months... and... are you sure you're feeling up to that? I don't think it's a good idea after what happened...'

I didn't know how to put into words what had happened mere hours previously. I was still shaken to the core with the fear of it and no matter how much Danny insisted the whole incident hadn't been as serious as I feared, I was still haunted by that feeling of complete and utter dread. The curtains swaying in the wind on the balcony. The sky lighting up with fireworks. That feeling of world-altering, unstoppable dread and panic lingering in the air around us.

But Pete told me it was a good sign that Danny wanted to be around his friends. He said it was good he wanted to see them and try to go back to normal. All talk of involving medical experts or therapists or medication could wait until the start of the new term, he assured me.

So I just went along with it.

My boy set off to his friend's house, Jonathan walking alongside him, with the plan that Pete would pick Danny up later to take him out for some dinner.

It was the last time I would ever see him alive.

I treated myself to a long bath that evening, before I knew anything was wrong, of course. I let the tension ebb away out of my body, the hot water gently lapping at my chin, the warm light complicated by a soothing silver-grey scented candle flickering on the little unit next to the bath. But any sense of calm I managed to achieve wasn't destined to last.

The hours went by and Pete and Danny didn't return.

I realised they would have a lot to talk about, which worried me in and of itself. What was Danny saying to his father?

As the minutes ticked on, I became more and more worried and began to text them – short 'just checking everything's fine' messages at first, followed by more panicked demands they call me or at least confirm they were OK. I pulled on a comfy tracksuit and padded barefoot down the stairs, phone clutched in my hand, and sat next to the Christmas tree, hoping I would hear the car on the drive outside at any moment.

I got no reply to my messages. They didn't even come up as read. I then worried about what situation Pete might have had to deal with when he'd got there.

It was all going wrong. I'd hoped the band practice and dinner would help Danny relax. Get back to normal. Work his way through whatever was going on with his friends. And this weird atmosphere between us all would have dissipated.

But of course that never happened.

I got the call from the police a few minutes later.

I can't really remember what they said, but the key words had me running to the front door, forgetting to put on my shoes. I clung on to the fact that they were alive – they were still alive! – otherwise the police wouldn't have phoned; they'd have visited. I just needed to get to the hospital.

That's all, I told myself. Just get to the hospital and they'd be there – perhaps a bit bruised, maybe a broken arm or two, but they'd be alive; they'd mend.

It would all be OK.

As soon as I'd got out of the house and aimed the keys at my car, I saw her. Janet Franklin, walking her mother's enormous Newfoundland dog, Charlton. On normal days I found it funny how bored the dog always looked in Janet's company, as if he, like the rest of us, was tired of her smug superiority and snobbish jibes and endless stories about why her children are amazing at anything they do. But on that evening, I couldn't see the dog's face. In the light from the street lamps and the Christmas lights tastefully adorning her house, I could only make out Janet's face looking at me as if I were insane, dashing out of my house in the freezing cold without shoes or a coat. And I didn't wait for her to say anything. I just shouted at her. Shouted the only thing I had on my mind, that I needed to let out, to tell someone, otherwise my overwhelming panic might swallow me whole. 'A crash!' I said. 'They've been in a crash.'

Of course, I realise how it must have sounded to Janet. Saying *they* must have made her instantly fear for the life of her own son. Because her boy, Jonathan, so often got a lift home with us. And I could see it in her face, all the fear and disorientation and horror that were rushing up inside of me.

'But… I thought the boys were together? Jonathan's not come home… Is he…? Where…?'

Then it all changed. Within a second, the whole situation was reframed, for Janet at least. Because her boy came running up to her out of nowhere, and we both stared at him.

'Oh my God!' she shouted and ran to him, putting her arms around him. 'Where the hell have you been?'

'I decided to run back from Scotty's,' he said to his mum, pulling away from her. 'I had my gym stuff on already.'

She continued to just stare at him, then came the relief. Even in the dim light I could see it fill her face as she stepped forwards and clutched him in her arms once more, leaving me to turn away and get into the car, letting waves of white-hot fury rush across me – fury at her for delaying me, for wasting this past minute or so, a minute that could have been vital.

It could have been. But it wasn't. Because they were dead by the time I reached the hospital. They'd died even before I'd put the key in the ignition.

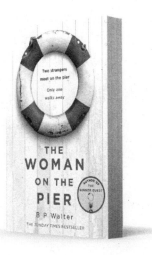

**Two strangers meet on the pier
Only one walks away…**

Screenwriter Caroline Byrne is desperate to know why her daughter Jessica died, murdered in Stratford when she was supposed to be at a friend's in Somerset.

When Caroline discovers the messages Jessica had been sending a boy named Michael, she realises it's because of him. Because he failed to meet her that day. He's the reason why her daughter is dead. And so she makes a choice. He's the one who's going to pay.
That is her promise. Her price.

Four people walked into the dining room that night. One would never leave.

Matthew: the perfect husband.
Titus: the perfect son.
Charlie: the perfect illusion.
Rachel: the perfect stranger.

Charlie didn't want her at the book club. Matthew wouldn't listen. And that's how Charlie finds himself slumped beside his husband's body, their son sitting silently at the dinner table, while Rachel calls 999, the bloody knife still gripped in her hand.

**If you go down to the woods today,
you're in for a big surprise...**

Kitty Marchland has always known that her family aren't like others. But when her father uproots them to a remote cottage in the woods, she realises that her parents are keeping secrets from her – secrets that could unravel everything.

Years later, Kitty starts to question what really happened out in the forest. When the police revisit a suspicious death, she must examine her most painful memories – and this time, there's nowhere to hide...

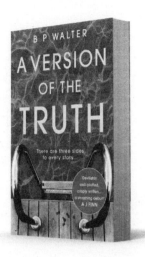

We all see what we want to see…

2019: Julianne is preparing a family dinner when her son comes to show her something on his iPad – something that will make her question everything about her marriage and turn her husband into a stranger.

1990: A fresher student at Oxford, Holly is well out of her depth when she falls into an uneasy friendship with a group of older students and begins to develop feelings for one in particular. He's confident, quiet, attractive, and seems to like her too. But she soon begins to realise she might just be a disposable pawn in a very sinister game.

ONE MORE CHAPTER

YOUR NUMBER ONE STOP FOR PAGETURNING BOOKS

The author and One More Chapter would like to thank everyone who contributed to the publication of this story...

Analytics
Emma Harvey
Maria Osa

Audio
Fionnuala Barrett
Ciara Briggs

Contracts
Georgina Hoffman
Florence Shepherd

Design
Lucy Bennett
Fiona Greenway
Holly Macdonald
Liane Payne
Dean Russell

Digital Sales
Laura Daley
Michael Davies
Georgina Ugen

Editorial
Arsalan Isa
Charlotte Ledger
Jennie Rothwell
Tony Russell
Caroline Scott-Bowden
Kimberley Young

International Sales
Bethan Moore

Marketing & Publicity
Chloe Cummings
Emma Petfield

Operations
Melissa Okusanya
Hannah Stamp

Production
Emily Chan
Denis Manson
Francesca Tuzzeo

Rights
Lana Beckwith
Rachel McCarron
Agnes Rigou
Hany Sheikh
Mohamed
Zoe Shine
Aisling Smyth

The HarperCollins Distribution Team

The HarperCollins Finance & Royalties Team

The HarperCollins Legal Team

The HarperCollins Technology Team

Trade Marketing
Ben Hurd

UK Sales
Yazmeen Akhtar
Laura Carpenter
Isabel Coburn
Jay Cochrane
Alice Gomer
Gemma Rayner
Erin White
Harriet Williams
Leah Woods

And every other essential link in the chain from delivery drivers to booksellers to librarians and beyond!

ONE MORE CHAPTER

One More Chapter is an
award-winning global
division of HarperCollins.

Subscribe to our newsletter to get our
latest eBook deals and stay up to date
with all our new releases!

signup.harpercollins.co.uk/
join/signup-omc

Meet the team at
www.onemorechapter.com

Follow us!

@OneMoreChapter_
@OneMoreChapter
@onemorechapterhc

Do you write unputdownable fiction?
We love to hear from new voices.
Find out how to submit your novel at
www.onemorechapter.com/submissions